CHAINLINK

Jordan and his riders kept pushing the thousand head of Arizona beef southward. Pushing them toward the vast, tawny, empty land known as the Big Bend. At the first camp in Texas Jordan bent and scooped up a handful of Texas dirt. He was home again. Home on Major Clay's crazy gamble— buying a bankrupt Big Bend ranch and stocking it with Arizona beef! The Major's money had bought Chainlink . . . but it was Griff Jordan's strength and savvy that would have to hold onto it.

OWEN EVENS

CHAINLINK

Complete and Unabridged

LINFORD
Leicester

First Linford Edition
published September 1988

British Library CIP Data

Evens, Owen
    Chainlink.—Large print ed.—
Linford western library
I. Title
823′.914[F]

ISBN 0-7089-6597-0

Published by
F. A. Thorpe (Publishing) Ltd.
Anstey, Leicestershire
Set by Rowland Phototypesetting Ltd.
Bury St. Edmunds, Suffolk
Printed and bound in Great Britain by
T. J. Press (Padstow) Ltd., Padstow, Cornwall

To Penny

1

BY the time they neared the Texas line Griff Jordan was used to the surprised comments and the jibes directed at the cattle drive he was ramrodding. Whenever Griff and his outfit skirted remote villages or isolated cow camps on their way south men would shout: "Hey, don't you fellas know that Kansas is north? You can't sell cows in Texas. You're headin' the wrong way!"

It was the old men who laid on the sarcasm, probably feeling that age held them immune from the tough-looking crew. The younger men silently speculated on the reason for twenty riders pushing southward a thousand head of Arizona beef. Pushing them not to Abilene and the cattle market, but toward the vast tawny empty land known as the Big Bend. There you couldn't sell beef for a Jeff Davis dollar, let alone good hard coin of the United States.

At the drag rumbled a chuckwagon and a canvas-topped wagon, both brand new when purchased in Tucson. Above the clatter of the

1

herd and the yells of the riders fighting strays came the sound of steady moaning and profanity from a man in the bed of the larger wagon.

Now and then Griff Jordan's brown gaze would drift toward the lurching wagon, and his big body would stiffen in the saddle. As the outfit crested a ridge and the cattle streamed down onto the lush grass of the Rio Basin, Griff reined his grulla over to the wagon.

But the moaning and the cursing had stopped. Griff swung in beside the driver, a giant of a man whose canvas jacket was split up the back from the pull of his enormous shoulders against the four-horse team.

"Remember what I told you, Wheat," Griff Jordan reminded him coldly. "Next time the major wants whisky you tell me. No more sneaking it from a peddler."

George Wheat stared down at him out of bloodshot eyes. His brows were a thick unbroken line across a narrow forehead. "The major's money bought this outfit," Wheat said shortly. "Not yours. Tell *him* about the whisky."

Griff held in his temper. Too much was riding on this venture to risk a showdown. He needed every man. But he made a mental note to fire the teamster-cook as soon as they reached the new ranch. "Give the men a decent meal tonight," Griff said, and eyed the big driver. "They've earned it."

He wheeled away into the dust, aware of a chill in his belly. Not put there from his scene with George Wheat, but because they were nearing the Texas line. It was still not too late to turn back, he told himself. But the thought vanished instantly: if he didn't ride his cards all the way for the blue chips, he was through. At thirty-one a man didn't get many chances for the big money. He meant to make the most of this one.

Griff Jordan knew the hour they crossed the Texas border. There was no marker, nothing to show that he was once again in the land of his birth. He stood tall in the stirrups, watching the stream of brown hides kick through the dust, remembering a distant day in Texas when hide was all a man could sell. "Bullhide" Jordan, they had called his father. The old man had made a fortune in hides before the war. He had lost that and much more when Texas pulled out of the Union.

The air smelled different to Griff as he tilted

back his bared head and let the Texas sun touch the shaggy mane of brown hair. The sky had more color here. And even the Arizona tobacco tasted better when you drew it deep into your lungs, for it was mixed with good Texas air.

At the first camp in Texas Griff set out the night guard and saw the cook fires begin their night blooming against the mesquites. Griff bent his tall body and scooped up a handful of dirt and let it trickle through his fingers. Texas dirt. Home again. Once he had been twenty-one, rushing north along this very trail. But that was a decade ago, a war ago. A lifetime ago.

Ed Damon, the slender one-eyed man Griff had named his segundo, came up from the shadows. "How long before we get where we're goin', Griff?"

"Not long."

"And the boss ain't even bought the land yet," Damon said, peering up at the foreman out of his good eye. The other eye was covered with a dusty black patch.

"The deal's all set," Griff said, and wished he felt as confident as he tried to sound. "Major Clay only has to sign the papers." He glanced at the big wagon pulled up at the edge of the campsite.

Damon, following his gaze, said, "I hope the major's steady enough to hold a pen."

"He'll sign," Griff said grimly, "if I have to hold his hand."

"Ain't no free range left in the Bend, so I hear," Ed Damon said. He was a worrier, a good man, but inclined to pack his job around on his shoulders like lead weights. He flung out a slim hand. "We got to have graze for them cows, Griff."

Griff nodded, and rubbed a hand wearily across his jaw. He had picked up this crew in Arizona, offering top money for the long and dangerous drive. And the other dangers they would face in the raw country known as the Bend. Major Milo Clay, who had spent the past days dead drunk in the wagon, might be short on will power when it came to the potency found in bottles, but he was generous with his new-found wealth. He paid top money.

"I hope the boss don't spend all his money the first year," Damon said, his good eye twinkling. "A man'd sure feel dirt poor on a regular ridin' job after workin' for the major."

"It would take a lot of years," said Griff, "for the boss to spend all his money."

"He really got a million dollars like they say?"

"The Comstock isn't as rich as it was before he cashed in his silver stocks and turned to ranching."

"You and him was in the war together, wasn't you, Griff?"

"We were both in the war," Griff said coolly.

Damon, realizing he had said something to nettle the foreman, changed the subject. "I'm sure sorry the major got hold of that whisky. And he ain't had a drink before that since we pulled outa Tucson." The major had really tied on the bear during their last night in the town.

Griff was staring across the camp ground at big George Wheat at the cook fire. He wondered now how he could have made a mistake in Wheat when he hand-picked this crew in Arizona. Pick a man for his size instead of his brains and you deserve what you get, Griff thought.

George Wheat's bellowing voice cut across the camp ground with its nightly attempt at humor: "Main dinin' room of the Bison Hotel in Dodge, now open for business."

Griff walked to where Wheat was serving up floured steaks and beans to the men not guarding the herd. The men began grumbling about the beans being sour. Griff shouldered up, sniffed at the bean pot sitting on the work board of the chuck wagon.

He straightened up and the men grew silent, watching. "Wheat, I told you the men deserved a good meal."

"Them beans ain't sour." Wheat had a tight ugly look in his cat-yellow eyes.

Griff felt a rush of anger. Ever since he had hired on this giant, he had sensed Wheat was out to cause trouble. Just a lot of little nagging things to make a dreary, rough cattle drive all the more miserable.

Griff threw the pot of beans into the fire. Then, resting a booted foot on a stump Wheat had used as a chopping block for kindling, he said, "Cook up something else, Wheat. I don't give a damn what it is. But make it something a man doesn't need a zinc-lined stomach to digest."

The men stood rigid, wondering if this would end up in a shooting or fists. If the latter happened they felt sorry for the boss. Big as he was, Griff Jordan was no match for the towering George Wheat.

Wheat put both big hands into the pockets of his canvas jacket. Damon, at Griff's elbow, warned, "He packs a derringer in one of them pockets. And a razor in the other."

Griff kicked at the fire and embers shot out, spraying the front of George Wheat's pants. With an oath, the big man leaped back, his hands jerking out of his pockets. Off balance, he caught the tailgate of the chuckwagon. And at that moment Griff had him by an arm, swinging with all his weight. George Wheat went to one knee and Griff levered on the arm and brought it down across the stump. Wheat shouted with pain.

With his tremendous strength, Wheat almost succeeded in getting to his feet, bringing Griff with him. But Griff fell on the arm with his full weight. Wheat sobbed in agony.

As Wheat struggled, Griff, sweating, said, "Ease off. I'll break it sure as hell. I mean it."

And Wheat ceased his thrashing, glaring at Griff from where he lay on the ground, his arm levered across the chopping block.

"Empty his pockets, Ed," Griff told his segundo.

In a moment Damon had fetched a one-shot derringer and a razor with a yellowed bone handle from Wheat's jacket.

Griff let up the pressure on the big man's arm and got to his feet. He picked up his hat, dusted it against his thigh. The men stood around, looking uneasy. You didn't fight a big man like George Wheat. If you had trouble with him you shot him. Their eyes said that their boss had an empty skull to try and wrestle a man the size of Wheat.

Rubbing his arm, Wheat clambered to his feet. He was sullen, and across one side of his face was a smear of dust.

Griff said, "I can't spare any riders for cook. But I will if I have to. You're hired to cook. If there's some reason you don't like this job you can draw your time."

For a moment Wheat only glared, then he said, "I'll have supper cooked in an hour."

He turned back to the cook fire and the men began to breathe easier.

"Why didn't you kick him out at the end of a rifle?" Ed Damon asked quietly.

"He's up to something," Griff said. "I'd like to know what it is before we get rid of him." He knew now he had been foolish in tangling with Wheat. But for a moment he'd lost his temper. He had learned long ago—or thought he had—that if violence threatened, the only thing to use was a gun.

"You watch out for him, Griff," Damon advised.

"If somebody hired him to sign on with this outfit," Griff said, watching Wheat industriously turning out a new meal, "I want to read his brand."

"He's the one gave the major that peddler whisky."

"I jumped him for it," Griff said. "He figured to get back at me by feeding us slop."

Griff walked to the canvas-topped wagon and leaned in at the tailgate. "How you feeling, Milo?" he asked the major.

"Like I'd been weaned on coal oil," a drawling voice replied. "What in God's name did I drink?"

"Peddler whisky. Someday it'll kill you."

Major Milo Clay sat up in the cavern made by high sideboards and canvas. In a shaft of light from the moon inching up over the hump of a hill, the major's face looked ghastly. "A drunkard's grave." He gave a shaky laugh. "A fine end for Major Milo Clay, late of the CSA."

"Don't rub it in, Milo," Griff said coldly. "Not the CSA part."

"Hell, I'm sorry, Griff." He braced his narrow back against a cowhide trunk. "I forget that the Confederate States of America no longer exist."

"We've made good time," Griff said, letting some of the stiffness ease off in his voice. "We'll be at Elvine's Store tomorrow."

Milo Clay slowly drew his hands away from his face. "But the last time I counted we were four days away—"

"And you've been four days dead drunk."

The major got that petulant look Griff knew so well. At the close of the war they'd lost track of each other for a time. But once on a trip to Virginia City from Elko, where he was working as foreman on a ranch, Griff ran into the major. The major was hoping to make the stake he had been constantly striving for since their brief association at the tag end of hostilities. The major wanted to become a rich man, not so much for himself but for his only kin, a niece living in Del Carmen, Texas. And he *had* become rich . . .

"You could have taken the jug away from

me," the major said, the petulant look more pronounced on his pale face.

"Once you start, you might as well let it run its course," Griff said. "Besides, I've got a herd to watch."

"You've known me a long time," Milo Clay said with a dry laugh. "You know my—shall we say—weaknesses."

"It isn't a laughing matter." Griff leaned close. "This isn't Virginia City, Milo. This is Texas. If anybody suspected what we carry in this wagon you'd have the back of your head blown off before you could whistle."

"You know what's in the wagon," the major said, and patted the wagon bed with the palm of his hand. "Maybe you could be rich all at once. With only a dead Milo Clay—"

"You know me better than that," Griff snapped. "But from now on you'd better stay sober."

"I wish I knew what makes me drink," the major said querulously.

"Afraid of the future?" Griff struck a match on the sideboards to light a cigar. In the brief flash he saw the sickness the cheap peddler rotgut had put in his friend's eyes. Suddenly he wanted to take a gunbarrel to George Wheat.

"What man isn't afraid of the future?" the major said when the match went out and darkness swept in around his slender figure. In the flare of light Griff had seen the stains on the expensive clothes of this man who, with his good manners, had managed to make influential friends in Virginia City. When there'd been a tip on the silver exchange he'd put every dime he could borrow on it. In one wild night the major had become a rich man.

And then he had written Griff Jordan, running the JB outfit out of Elko . . . *The worthless life you saved in the war is now of considerable value. You've always wanted to go back to Texas and so have I. Here is your chance. As my partner. Meet me at the Washoe Hotel on the fifteenth of the month and we'll discuss details . . .*

Griff said, "Use your razor tomorrow and get yourself cleaned up. You sign the Chainlink papers with Leithbut in the morning."

Again the major patted the planks of the wagon bed. "I feel rather sorry for Leithbut. He's the one who could be getting the back of his head blown out."

"A man who wants cash instead of a check has to take the risks." Griff leaned in and put

13

a hand on the major's thin shoulder. "How about some food?" And when the major shook his head, Griff added, "You want to be stone sober when you see your niece in a day or so—"

"My niece," the major said, and looked away. "Maydelle Ashley. My only reason for this grand excursion back to Texas."

Griff frowned, wondering at the major's reaction every time the name of his niece was mentioned. Earlier in the year the major had made a trip by himself to Del Carmen. When he returned to Tucson where Griff was buying a herd and hiring men, he said he had made secret negotiations to buy the bankrupt Chainlink ranch from a man named Leithbut. But he didn't mention seeing his niece. Griff didn't press the matter. He had the feeling the major didn't want to discuss the girl whom he hadn't seen since she was a baby.

"My one ambition, Griff," the major said. "To give this girl the things she's been denied up to now. I intend to make her the cattle queen of West Texas. And then be damned to them—" The major's voice broke off.

Griff said, "I'll send George Wheat over with some black coffee."

"That bastard," Milo Clay said under his breath.

"Whose idea was it about the whisky? His or yours?"

"He bought the jug from the peddler. Letting me sniff it was like putting raw meat in a wolf trap."

Griff tramped away and halted near the bedground, staring at the dark irregular line of the hills. There was a coldness in his belly not altogether due to the fact that after ten years he was home and ready to take whatever his fellow Texans thought he deserved. The coldness was also because of the uncertainty of what lay ahead. Because in the war he had saved the life of the man in the wagon, he was now being offered a partnership. A quarter interest in a thousand head of beef. A quarter interest in Chainlink, the old Benbow ranch.

From the first it had seemed incredible that the Benbows would sell Chainlink. A lot of blood had dried on Chainlink dust during past attempts to wrest control of the ranch from the family. But the man now selling it was not a Benbow. This Leithbut had foreclosed on Chainlink when Tom Benbow, the older brother, had been killed.

As Griff turned for the cook fire he vowed nobody would spoil this opportunity. Already he had missed too many. A man didn't make his stake ramrodding a spread like the JB in Elko. No, he had to own beef. That's where the money was.

And because Major Milo Clay wanted to sweep into Texas like a Caesar back from the wars, he had insisted they come with a herd of beef. "To kick up a little dust and let the natives know they're dealing with a rich man, not a one-dollar lawyer on a ten-dollar saddle. Which is the way I left Texas. And I want them to know I'm the uncle of Maydelle Ashley."

Tears had come to Milo Clay's eyes when he said the last. "People respect a rich man. They'll respect his rich niece."

2

THE next morning when they were ready to move out, George Wheat clambered to the wagon seat and whipped up the four-horse team. The horses surged into their collars, struggling to pull the big wheels out of deep sand.

When the wagon was rolling, Wheat looked down as Griff Jordan swung back from the herd. "This is the heaviest damn load I ever seen," he complained slyly. "Only carryin' me and the major and a trunk. One of us must have a ton of weight that don't show."

Griff's brown face did not change expression. "You tend to your driving and forget the rest."

Wheat grunted under his breath, then flexed his right arm. "Got a sore arm this mornin'," he said, his cat-yellow eyes hard on Griff's face. "Must've slept on it wrong."

"Lucky you didn't get it broken," Griff said. He waited for the wagon to pass, then rode up to the tailgate and looked in. Milo Clay, looking some better than he had last night, was putting on a clean shirt.

"We'll sight Elvine's Store about noon," Griff shouted above the rattle of the groaning wagon wheels. "How's your hand? Steady?"

Milo Clay smiled. "Steady enough to sign us into an eighty-thousand dollar ranch, amigo."

Griff felt a surge of excitement. An eighty-thousand dollar ranch, a thousand head of beef. And a part of each would be his.

Clay crawled to the tailgate. "I overheard our mountain of a whisky procurer complaining about the weight of the wagon. Think he suspects anything?"

"He won't be with us long," Griff told the major.

"It'll be Leithbut's worry in another few hours."

Elvine's Store, a rambling structure built of twelve-by-twelve timbers, was a place where a man with a posse eating his dust could swap horses or buy a rifle or anything else to ease his escape into Mexico. Despite its unsavory reputation Leithbut had insisted the papers transferring title of Chainlink should be signed here. Not in Del Carmen. When the deal was set up Griff thought it odd, but this was the major's show all the way. If Major Clay was satisfied, he'd go along.

Slightly before noon Griff followed the heavy wagon away from the herd after telling Ed Damon to keep the cattle moving south.

Dick Elvine, the store's proprietor, met them in the yard. He was a spindly-legged man who looked more like a schoolteacher than he did the proprietor of such a notorious outpost. But he was supposed to be honest, and if he gave his word he'd keep it.

"Are you Major Clay?" Elvine asked as Griff dismounted.

"The major's coming in the wagon." Griff pointed at the heavy vehicle lumbering up through the dust. "We're supposed to meet a man named Leithbut."

"He's waiting inside," Elvine said. "Impatiently, I might add." Elvine gave a dry laugh and nodded at two men lounging by a corral some distance away. The men were eyeing Griff. "Leithbut's bodyguards. Did you bring the money?"

Griff looked at Elvine's eyes behind the steel-rimmed eyeglasses. "You seem to be a curious man. I'd heard different."

"It isn't every day the Benbow ranch is sold."

Elvine peered at the approaching wagon. "My God! That's George Wheat driving!"

"You know him?"

"No friend of mine. Last time he was around here he left rather unexpectedly."

This was interesting but before Griff could question Elvine about Wheat, a lathy, excited man in a wrinkled gray suit burst from the store. It was Leithbut and when he learned the major was arriving in the wagon, a little color returned to a haggard, fear-ridden face. He scampered to meet the wagon.

"He's nervous," Griff drawled. "He sleep on an ant hill last night?"

"You'd be nervous too if you were selling Chainlink," Elvine said.

"Why?" Griff gave Elvine a hard speculative stare.

"The Benbows won't be happy."

"They no longer own Chainlink. Leithbut does."

"And he's worrying about it."

Now the major was out of the wagon, shaking hands with Leithbut. When they went into the store together to complete the transaction, Griff walked to the wagon where George Wheat lounged against a wheel. Griff had ordered him to tie a saddler to the tailgate this morning. Now he told Wheat to cut the horse loose and ride back to the herd and take Ed Damon's orders. Without a word Wheat turned his wide back and tramped back to the horse. In a moment he was riding out.

Griff went into the store where Leithbut and the major were seated at a table, scanning legal-looking documents. The store had a short bar, shelves of tinned goods, some deal tables and a few rooms for overnight guests. Elvine leaned against his bar, drinking his own whisky.

When the papers were signed by the major, Leithbut pushed across a receipt for the money to be paid for Chainlink. He was sweating. "You brought the—I mean you got it with you?" Leithbut stammered.

The major smiled and winked at Griff. "Just sign, Mr. Leithbut. And you'll have possession of the *wagon*."

Major Clay beckoned to Leithbut and the two of them went outside and around to the back of the wagon. In a few moments they returned. Leithbut's eyes were shining. He hastily signed a receipt. He was preparing to leave when there was a sudden surge of hoofbeats in the yard.

From a side window Griff saw three tough-looking men and a pretty girl rein in and dismount. The girl signalled the men and they stayed behind with the horses. She hurried toward the store. Griff could tell from her agitation that she was worked up about something.

Inside the store she halted a moment to adjust her gaze from sunlight to gloom. Griff saw a tall girl wearing about her throat a blue scarf that matched her eyes. Her shirt was a faded blue as were her canvas breeches. She wore scuffed boots. Although her femininity spoke from every curve and swell in the tight-fitting clothes, Griff got the impression that she could handle a horse like a man and probably play a man's game at cards.

Leithbut was on his feet, holding out his hands and looking scared. "Lisa Benbow—"

Her eyes swung to the major, who stood up. Although he had sobered there was a noticeable tremor in his limbs. "You're Major Clay?"

"At your service, ma'am."

"There was a letter came for my brother. I took the liberty of opening it. It said you and Leithbut were going to transact business here at this appointed hour." She gave him a scornful look.

"I knew Clyde Benbow had a sister," the major said. "I had no idea she was such a beauty."

Despite the tenseness of the moment Lisa Benbow flushed and clenched her hands. "I am asking you a favor. Don't buy Chainlink!"

Major Milo Clay put his hands on the top of the table to still their trembling. "Your brother sent you," he accused.

She shook her pale head. "My brother Clyde has one object in life. He wants to own Chainlink again. He wants to restore it to the great ranch it was when my father was alive."

"A commendable ambition," the major said, "but—"

"There must be other ranches for sale in Texas," she implored.

"I've settled on Chainlink," the major said stiffly and, with his hands clenched behind his back, he walked to a window and stood peering out at the dust cloud kicked up by the herd in the distance.

Lisa whirled on Leithbut, who licked his lips and said, "Lisa, you've got to understand. I couldn't turn down this offer—"

"Clyde asked you to wait until he raised the money in Kansas," Lisa said. Her face was white. Griff, watching her blue eyes, saw she was not only enraged, but scared. "Clyde *told* you to wait," she stormed.

Leithbut was hanging onto the edge of the table as if threatened with collapse. "Clyde offered me thirty thousand," he said hoarsely. "The major paid me eighty."

Lisa's brow lifted. The rise and fall under the blue fabric of her shirt was slowly stilled as she fought to control her breathing. "I hope you realize some happiness from your enormous profit," she said, trying to be sarcastic, but failing. She closed her eyes, opened them. "Don't you know that Clyde will be furious?"

Leithbut said, "By the time Clyde gets back from Kansas I'll be in Frisco—"

"Clyde wrote me that he's on his way home. That was weeks ago. He'll be back any day."

Leithbut looked as if somebody had put a cocked gun at his head.

While he slowly paled, Lisa crossed the store to where Major Clay stood with his back to her. "My brother won't take this kindly, Major Clay. If you knew him you'd realize—"

Griff saw the major wheel, his face white.

"I've never had the pleasure of knowing him. Only knowing of some of the things he's done." He gave her a withering look and Lisa Benbow, obviously confused, backed up a step.

She bit her lip, then turned for the door and Griff noticed the golden rope of hair held at the back of her neck by a thick ring of Spanish silver. He followed her outside. "You think there'll be trouble over the major buying Chainlink?"

She gave him a sidelong glance out of her blue eyes. "Trouble? Yes, I should say you can call it that."

She started away and he caught her by an arm and swung her around. "Tell your brother to think twice about starting trouble." Then, at the indignation in her eyes, he added in a softer tone, "Miss Benbow, if a man can't hold a ranch he isn't entitled to it. I'm sorry. For your sake."

The moment he touched her the three men waiting by the horses came forward, their spurs ringing. A tough trio. A big sandy-haired man and a black-haired one, and one who might have been handsome save for a scarred mouth, this one looking as if a knife blade had once ripped from lip to jawbone. They halted a few feet away, but still Griff did not let go of Lisa's arm. He was feeling the soft-hard woman muscle under the thin sleeve of her shirt. He didn't want to let go of her.

Lisa knocked Griff's hand from her arm and said to the black-haired one, who seemed to be the leader, "Never mind, Keller. He won't touch me again."

She turned and gave Griff a long measuring look, then went toward her horse. The black-haired Keller spat, staring at Griff out of hard gray eyes. "Don't touch her when Clyde gets home, mister. Don't even look at her."

As they turned for their horses George Wheat came suddenly around a corner of the store and practically ran into them. Wheat gave Lisa such a hungry look that he appeared ridiculous.

Keller said, "Well, if it ain't George Wheat." He jerked a thumb at Griff standing rigid in the center of the yard, and said, "Don't tell me you're workin' for his two-bit outfit."

Wheat went on staring at Lisa and after a moment she turned and gave the big man a wavering smile. "What are you doing back in Texas, George?"

Griff came up swiftly and halted behind Lisa. His eyes locked with Wheat's. Without looking

26

at the girl he said, "I'm glad one of our crew gets a welcome to Texas, anyway."

She turned to peer up at Griff. "Yes, I'll welcome back the man who used to cook for us. I won't welcome you, however." She walked toward her horse, giving Wheat a studied look as she passed. "You'd better keep out of Clyde's way," she warned in a low voice. But Griff heard her, and frowned. So there was a connection between George Wheat and Clyde Benbow . . .

When the girl and the three men had ridden out, Griff turned on Wheat. "I told you to stay with the herd."

"My hoss got a loose shoe. I come back."

Griff's smile was hard. "I'd like to take the time to hear about your years with the Benbows. But I'm busy with other things. Wheat, you're fired. Don't bother to pick up your gear. I'll have it sent to Del Carmen."

Without a word Wheat walked off. In a moment he rode a big dun savagely out of the clearing and disappeared in the cottonwoods. Griff figured the man wanted to be fired.

When Griff turned again for the store he saw Elvine standing by the door. "Clyde Benbow ran Wheat out once," Elvine said, polishing his glasses on his shirt sleeve. "Surprised he'd come back." When Griff started into the store, Elvine said, "Wheat has quite a reputation as a brawler in these parts. The only man who ever lived after tangling with him hasn't walked since. That was two years ago."

"A big tough man is a little dead man when he's got a bullet in him," Griff said.

Leithbut was anxious to move on. With his two bodygards whom he introduced as the Oakum brothers, he figured to drive the rest of the day and most of the night. "Don't buy all of Frisco at the first jump," Griff said. "Save a little of it for later."

Leithbut looked grim. "Between you and me I ain't goin' to Frisco. It's Mexico. And I'm leavin' right now!"

When the outfit had moved off, the heavily-laden wagon lurching in the ruts, the Oakum brothers riding guard, the major reflected on one man's fear of another. "Benbow has him scared right out of his hair," Clay said. Then he looked up at Griff's grim face. "Why'd you fire Wheat?"

"Several reasons. One of them was the fact that the Benbow girl said she opened a letter addressed to her brother."

28

Major Clay's reddish brows lifted. "You think Wheat wrote Benbow we were going to be at Elvine's Store on this date?"

"I'll bet my sour socks on it." Griff swore softly, remembering that Elvine said George Wheat had once been run out by Benbow. And now Wheat was trying to do Benbow a favor. Well, this wasn't the only puzzle.

"You stay away from Wheat," the major said worriedly. "I need you whole. Not with your skull caved in by his boots."

"And you stay away from whisky. This isn't Virginia City with frock coats and beaver hats. This is Texas."

"I promise, Griff." The major planned to take the afternoon stage for the county seat at Del Carmen where he would record the deed for Chainlink. Griff suggested he go along but the major said Griff would be busy the next few days pushing the herd onto Chainlink. With a pointed stick he drew a rough map of Chainlink boundaries.

When this was done the major said he was going to nap in one of the rooms Elvine kept for overnight guests, until the stage arrived.

When Major Clay had gone to the room Griff bought himself a drink at Elvine's bar. Lord, he felt tired. It had been a long gruelling drive east and then south. And he'd added a few enemies to the ones he knew would be waiting for him now that he was back in Texas. If the story of his return was told to the right people, that was.

He had made an enemy of Wheat, and the three men with Lisa Benbow would probably do anything Clyde Benbow suggested to harrass Chainlink's new owners. And the girl certainly hadn't looked on him with favor. Touching her arm and holding it had been a damn fool trick. Men had been shot for less, putting their hand on a woman they didn't even know. But something had compelled him. And he tried to recapture the surge of warmth that brief touch had brought to him.

Elvine said across his bar, "Funny thing, now I think of it, but I didn't see no money change hands when the major and Leithbut signed their papers."

Griff finished his drink. "That so?"

Elvine grew uneasy under Griff's steady gaze. "I only meant that it seems loco to carry eighty thousand dollars around in a wagon."

"That's the way Leithbut wanted it." Griff leaned close. "Keep that under your hat,

Elvine. Or maybe you won't have a head to hang the hat on."

"I ain't seen nothin', I ain't heard nothin'. That's how come I've been able to stay here this long."

"Then you better practice that philosophy."

"Yeah. But it ain't every day a wagonload of money rolls into your yard. Where was it hid? False bottom in the wagon bed—"

Griff said, "It's Leithbut's worry now. Maybe he'll wish before it's over that he was a man who trusted banks."

"Shouldn't wonder."

"And don't get any ideas of telling Clyde Benbow about it," Griff said.

"Mister, I wouldn't give Clyde Benbow the manure scrapin's off my boots." He bent over and rolled up a pants leg. "Clyde done that to me when he was younger. With them big Mex spurs of his."

Griff leaned over the bar and saw an ugly gash along Elvine's shinbone. "Seems Benbow's a man with a temper."

"I wouldn't give him no more credit. So that's what he done to me." Elvine rolled down the pants leg. "Tom Benbow was a right nice fella. And Miss Lisa is nice. But the old man was a hellion. And Clyde must sleep on the old man's grave of a night, because every year he gets meaner than a ruttin' bull. Only person he shows any feelin' for at all is his sister Lisa."

Griff said, "You've been around here a long time. Ever hear of a girl in Del Carmen named Maydelle Ashley?"

Elvine gave a short laugh. "Why sure. Every man with long pants in this end of Texas knows Maydelle. Why?"

Griff started to press the matter, but then decided that he'd already courted trouble enough for one day. And he felt a complete index to the character of Maydelle Ashley would add more obstacles to the job of establishing a ranch in the Bend.

From his half-open door the major watched Griff spur out of the yard, riding in the direction taken by the new Chainlink herd. For a long moment Major Milo Clay, late of the CSA, stood with a look of dejection on his face. Although he was fifty he had prided himself that he didn't look it. Now as he glanced at his reflection in a cracked looking glass on the wall of his room he knew otherwise. Since his visit to Texas months ago, to set up a deal for a ranch, age had come in on him like an engulfing wave.

The whisky he had once consumed for pleasure was now a necessity. He moved along a narrow corridor and into the store. Elvine, behind his bar, looked up. And the major hesitated only a moment. "Whisky," he said.

The fifth drink destroyed his disgust at himself. He called on Elvine for a deck of cards which was quickly supplied. He played solitaire for a time, then talked Elvine into playing two-handed stud.

"You're pretty drunk," Elvine said. He might be the proprietor of an establishment with an unsavory reputation but he was above taking money from a man as drunk as the major. He let the major win a little, lose a little so that the game remained even.

"It's Griff's fault I'm drunk," the major said thickly, feeling sorry for himself. "I overheard him mention Maydelle. That's what started me drinkin'."

Elvine put down his cards. "She a friend of yours?"

"She's my neesh—" It took two tries before he could manage "niece."

Elvine looked at him and then shook his head, and said something under his breath.

There was the sound of horses in the yard and Elvine got up and looked out the window. It was the trio who had been with Lisa Benbow earlier.

The black-haired Keller swaggered in, followed by the sandy-haired Macready and Art Lawler with the scarred mouth. "We're lookin' for the gent that put his hand on Miss Benbow. The big fella. Chainlink ramrod."

Elvine spread his hands. "Jordan's gone."

"Who the hell is this?" Keller said, nodding at the major.

Elvine told him who it was and Keller got a tight grin on his lips and winked at the others. "Looks like the major is a card-playin' man, boys. Elvine, get him another bottle. I aim to set in with this gamblin' man."

Elvine hesitated while the major stared owlishly at the newcomers. "This smells bad to me, Keller," Elvine said worriedly, and glanced out the window. There were only three horses in the yard. "Did Lisa send you back?"

"We ride for Clyde, we don't ride for her,"

34

Keller said, and sat down at the table with the major.

"We unhorsed her back a ways," Macready said with a laugh. "By the time she gets saddled up again we'll be through here, eh, Keller?"

Keller took the cards from the major's trembling hands. He ran through the deck and then cursed. "You got five aces in this deck! You're a damn card slick!" He lunged out of his chair and threw the deck of cards into the face of the bewildered major. "Get a gun loose, or by damn I'll blow you out the window!"

Major Clay took a faltering backward step and held wide his hands. "I'm unarmed."

Elvine said, "Keller, this is murder!"

"Not if you ain't a witness."

Elvine gave him a hard grin that belied the innocent eyes behind the spectacles. "Even you're not that crazy."

Keller holstered the black-butted gun he had drawn and began to roll up his sleeves. "If you ain't wearin' a gun, major," he said, softly, "I reckon I'll have to teach you manners another way." He looked up at Elvine. "How long since you mopped this floor?"

"Last week."

"You're gettin' it mopped now!" Keller reached for the major.

Lisa Benbow, who had finally got a saddle on the horse they had stripped, broke up the beating. When she saw the bleeding major on the floor, she beat at Keller's chest with her fists: "I told you not to come! I don't want bloodshed! Can't you get that through your stupid head?"

"It's what Clyde'd want me to do," Keller muttered, and picked up his hat. He took one look at the slightly-built man who lay unconscious on the floor, then jerked his head at his companions. "We'll wait an' ride back to the 'Little Place' with you," Keller told Lisa Benbow. But she wasn't listening.

Elvine was carrying the major into a back room and Lisa was hurrying to stoke the stove and put water on to heat. Keller and the two men went outside to wait.

It was later that the stage rolled in and Elvine gave the driver a message for Griff Jordan. "Sam, the herd may be strung along the road. If you see it, shoot off your rifle and get Jordan. If you don't see him leave a message in town for him."

36

"What about tellin' Sheriff Enright?"

"If you tell him," Elvine said soberly, "leave my name out of it."

The stage whirled off down the road that twisted through the cottonwoods.

3

AN hour later Griff got the message from the stage driver, who fired his rifle and almost spooked the herd before Griff rode over to find out what the trouble was. Telling Ed Damon to keep the herd moving south and east, Griff thanked the driver and headed at a hard run back toward Elvine's Store. According to the driver, the major was drunk and had been beaten up by the Benbow crowd.

What if they had gotten away with the deed for Chainlink? And as he spurred through the trees he cursed himself for trusting the major to stay sober.

Winded, concerned for the major's safety, Griff swung down in the yard, not seeing the three men lounging back in the cottonwoods.

He stormed in and saw Elvine pouring himself a drink at his bar. "Thanks for getting him drunk," Griff said through his teeth.

Elvine shook his head. "One man don't get

another drunk. The major knew what he wanted."

Griff listened while Elvine patiently explained what had happened.

"You could have stopped it," Griff shot at him.

Elvine gave a dry laugh. "Them three are tough boys. Besides, I'm already goin' pretty far on your side of the fence, Jordan. If I horned in on Keller—Well, I done enough gettin' you back here."

Griff bit back his temper and thanked Elvine for what he had done. Then he went to a back room where the major lay on a cot, a steaming towel wrapped around his face. Griff bent over the cot and removed the towel, and felt a flash of rage as he saw the swollen, purple features that he hardly recognized. He dropped the towel.

The major's eyes flickered open and he lay for a moment staring up at Griff through the swollen lids. Then he beckoned Griff closer and Griff bent down. The major put a hand under the mattress and by shifting his body was able to draw out a stiffened sheet of paper.

"The deed. I knew I was going to get drunk. I hid it."

Griff sighed. One problem, at least, had been solved. He sat on the edge of the cot. "Keller will pay for this, Milo. Elvine told me all about it."

The major closed his eyes and managed to shake his head. "Forget it, Griff. My fault. The Lord knows your return to Texas is hazardous enough, without adding to it."

"My return is my problem," Griff said thinly. "But so is Chainlink my problem." There was the sound of a woman's quick step and then Lisa Benbow came into the room carrying a jar of salve. She seemed surprised to see Griff.

"Nice work, Miss Benbow," he said coldly.

"I had nothing to do with it." She put the salve on a shelf.

"Next time you want a man whipped," he said, not believing her, "send your boys after *me*!"

She turned, straightening her shoulders. "Can't you be thankful the major isn't dead? If he'd been wearing a gun they might have shot him."

"You're the one who should be thankful he's not dead," Griff said thinly. "Because if he was, I'd start working on the Benbows with a rope."

Her chin lifted. "And I suppose you'd hang me?"

He looked at her, the grooves about his mouth as white as bleached bone.

Tearfully she told him what had happened, how Keller had pulled the saddle from her horse and then returned to Elvine's Store. "I begged them not to do it. But they thought it was what Clyde would want." She looked away, dashing tears from her eyes with the back of her hand.

"Your brother must pay high," Griff said. "Or maybe he has other means for commanding such loyalty." He went to the door and asked Elvine if he had a wagon to rent. Elvine said he had.

"You shouldn't move the major," Lisa said.

"Better he is moved," Griff said icily, "than lie here and risk a Benbow bullet in his head while he sleeps."

She recoiled as if he had slapped her. Angrily he tromped after Elvine, who intended showing him the wagon behind the barn. But Elvine drew up near the door and Griff nearly ran into him. Beyond Elvine's shoulder Griff saw Keller and his two friends, with their heads together near the cottonwoods. An oath escaped Griff, he checked the loads in his gun.

Elvine said, "I can't butt in no more, Jordan. If you call them three you're on your own." Griff shoved his gun back in its holster without reply. He was staring at the trio coming forward now to study Griff's horse and talk in low tones. Elvine added, "If you're bound to tangle, watch out for Keller. He's snake-quick with a gun."

Griff started around Elvine and Lisa hurried forward, her eyes pleading. "Don't," she begged. "This is what I'm trying to avoid."

Griff turned and looked at her stricken face, wondering whether to believe her. Maybe she was just a pretty woman, using her looks to make a man careless so when he turned his back one day her brother Clyde could put a knife in it.

He went out into the yard and the three men moved away from his horse and spread out a little. Keller stood with his feet spread, a slanted grin on his face. Macready edged away a half dozen yards from Keller's left. Art Lawler spat out of his scarred mouth and moved to the right. Griff's horse, sensing the tension, began to dance sideways, trying to avoid stepping on the trailed reins.

Griff eyed the black-haired, grinning Keller. "If you've got the guts," Griff said in a cold, deadly voice, "take off your gun. Have your partners take off theirs. Put the guns in the store where you can't get to them. I'll take you alone, Keller, or I'll take on the three of you."

"Tough talk," Keller said, and shot a glance at Lisa Benbow in the doorway. "You better get back inside, Miss Benbow."

"Keller, I'm ordering you to get out of here," Lisa said coldly.

Keller shook his head. "I told you once today. We work for Clyde. We don't work for you. Grab her, Elvine, and hold her while we finish this little business."

Griff did not dare turn his head, but he heard the sounds of a scuffle and knew Elvine probably had Lisa by the wrists. Elvine was saying, "Easy, Miss Benbow, easy," and she was screaming, "Keller, I *order* you!"

Keller ignored her and Griff said, "What is it, a gun or knuckles?"

"I ain't fist fightin' you, mister."

"You fought my partner."

"He was a damn cheat with five aces in the deck."

"You're the damn cheat."

"Careful, mister. Your partner wasn't wearin' a gun. It's the only thing that saved him from gettin' his hide hung on the fence for good."

Macready, the sandy-haired one, said nervously, "Maybe we better drift at that, Keller." He eyed the struggling Lisa Benbow, fighting to get free of Elvine. It was all the slightly-built store owner could do to hold her.

Lawler added his voice. "The gal might get hit, accidental, Keller. Clyde would burn you belly to backbone with a hot coal if anything happened to his sister."

Keller shrugged and said, "All right. We'll ride her back to the 'Little Place'—"

"I won't ride with you!" Lisa screamed. "I wouldn't ride with you if—"

She never finished it, for Keller suddenly swung on his heel and turned toward his horse as if to walk toward it. But he didn't. He continued to pivot, making a full circle. And as he swung around sunlight briefly struck the long barrel of the revolver he had drawn when his back was turned.

Only an instinct for such treachery saved Griff. His gun came up, crashing. Keller's eyes flew open in surprise as the first bullet shattered his collarbone. But the tremendous shock did not dislodge the gun from his fingers. As he tried to fire, the second bullet caught him high in the left side and ripped in toward his heart upon striking bone. He was dead before he struck the ground.

A vacuum of silence caught up all sound in the yard and held it. Only the scream of a jay and the far off rushing echoes of the gunfire. And Lisa Benbow standing rigid in the doorway, Elvine no longer holding her. And Macready, his gun half-drawn, staring down at Keller lying in the crooked-legged sprawl of death. Lawler's scarred mouth was taut so that the old knife wound seemed to be pulling his lips into a smile. There was no smile in his eyes as he turned his stunned gaze from the dead man to Griff Jordan.

"Jeez," he whispered, and looked at Macready.

Still holding his gun, Griff stepped back. "Draw it," he told Macready, "or drop it!"

Macready slowly closed his mouth that had opened in surprise at the sudden outcome of the gunplay. He looked down at his right hand that held the gun half out of leather. He took one dazed look at Griff, drew out the weapon the full distance to clear the holster. But carefully.

Very carefully. He made sure the tall, brown-faced man, hat on the back of his head, did not misinterpret the move. He let the gun fall.

Lawler, after only a moment's hesitation, added his weapon to the dust at Macready's feet. Without a word Griff backed around to their three horses. Keeping his eyes on the two men Griff fumbled for booted rifles and pulled them free and threw them into the cottonwoods.

"Get out," Griff said coldly. He jerked his revolver at the dead Keller. "Take him with you. My respects to Clyde Benbow."

"Mister," Lawler said hoarsely, "Clyde will kill you for this. Sure as hell, you'll be planted with Benbow lead in you."

"You tell Benbow to come himself next time."

"He'll come," Lawler predicted. "You don't need to worry about that."

When the body was roped to a horse and the two men were in the saddle, Lawler looked back. "You comin', Miss Benbow?"

She said nothing. She just stared at Griff Jordan. At the brown eyes pinched a little at the corners, at the full mouth also pinched. The curved jut of bone that was the nose. Tall and big through the shoulders, with the only move-

46

ment a slight stirring of his shirt from the breath he seemed barely to draw, as he watched Lawler and Macready ride out.

When they were gone, Lisa said, "You could have stopped it." She accused Griff.

"I suppose." Griff looked at her. "By letting Keller shoot me it could have been stopped."

"No."

"By me being dead instead of Keller." He jacked out the two spent shells. They lay in the dust beside Keller's hat, two gleaming cylinders of brass that had recently held the lead and powder that had taken a man's life.

Lisa's mouth quivered. "I begged Major Clay not to buy Chainlink. I begged him!"

"Excuse me," he said in a mild voice. "I understood Texas was in the Union. I didn't know a Benbow owned the state. I thought a man had a right to buy and sell."

"It was our ranch—once." Her voice trailed away. She seemed bewildered and frightened and not at all sure of what she should do next.

"I already told you," Griff said. "What a man can't hold he deserves to lose."

"I hope when your time comes, Mr. Jordan, you remember that." She rushed to her horse, flung herself into the saddle and spurred out of the yard. He could tell by the way her shoulders shook that she was crying.

Slowly Griff holstered his gun. He felt sick and mean and ugly. A girl had stood transfixed while he let a man draw his gun and then beat him to the shot. Shooting him so a piece of his collarbone leaped from his flesh like a broken trap spring. Shooting him again in the chest so that she could hear the sound the bullet made as it tore its jagged path into the heart. Whenever they met in the future she would be seeing him as the man who had done this bloody thing. Not thinking he had saved his own life. Remembering only the worst of it. And suddenly, in the moment she turned from him and he saw her gleaming hair and the straight line of her back and the hips marching under the canvas pants, he felt a stirring. Not the sensual cloud of heat that smothered a man when he had been too long with horses and cattle and too long without women. It was a gentle bubble of pain and desire crossing his heart. A desire to hold something and call up all the gentleness he thought he had buried forever in some forgotten year when he decided marriage was not for him. A thing that made a man think, and remember why he had been born. The need to live on through his sons . . .

Elvine came up and said, "Funny, but I usually hear of the good ones."

Griff turned. "The good ones?"

"The ones who can shoot like that. But I don't recollect the name of Griff Jordan icing a man's tongue when he says it aloud."

"There's a lot of talent undiscovered," Griff said bitterly. "Still unburied."

"Don't hold it against Lisa. This wasn't her doing."

"It was a Benbow doing. She's a Benbow."

"She's seen a lot of killing, Jordan."

"She saw another today," he said.

"Keller dying won't break her heart. But she saw her brother Tom and before that her poppa. They died the tough way." Elvine spat. "You and your partner have bought yourselves a war."

"I'll rent that wagon, Elvine, and get the major to Chainlink. He'll be safer there."

4

THAT afternoon Clyde Benbow, ruining a good horse in his fast ride down from Kansas, arrived in Del Carmen. His big handsome figure coated with dust, Benbow threw a dollar to a boy and told him to take the horse to the livery. Then he waved a hand at the crowd that had gathered to watch his return and bounded up the steps to the porch of the Del Carmen House hotel and bar. He came to an abrupt halt as Doctor Edmund Purcell came out of the hotel and observed the lathered, beaten horse the boy was leading away.

"It'd be a kindness to shoot the horse," Purcell said to Benbow, "instead of grain it. You've ruined a good animal, Clyde."

Clyde Benbow had removed his dirt-encrusted hat to beat it against the porch railing. "Like I've ruined everything else, Doc?" he said with a thin smile. Benbow towered over the fat doctor whose vest this early afternoon showed gravy stains, his white shirt rings of perspiration. Last night's whisky still

50

showed red in Purcell's eyes. The doctor often said that living in this "mote on the palm of God's hand known as the Big Bend will bring out any vice a man thought he had carefully buried."

Benbow removed from his pocket an oilskin packet and waved it under the doctor's nose. Benbow's white teeth gleamed and his hard gray gaze slid to the crowd on the walk below that had drifted up to witness the return of the last male Benbow to Del Carmen.

"A beef contract, Doc!" Benbow said loudly. "From a Chicago packing house. I had to go all the way to Kansas to get it, but here she is."

"You're a little late, Clyde," Purcell said.

Benbow shook his head. "It's never too late for a Benbow. I told you, by God, I'd get Chainlink back."

"A beef contract won't buy Chainlink."

"As soon as Leithbut turns Chainlink back to me, this packing house will pay him off. And Leithbut will loan me money for a herd and—"

"Leithbut sold out while you were gone."

Benbow, who had brushed past the doctor to enter the hotel, now wheeled back. His features were set in an ugly pattern and at the moment there was little trace of the good looks that so many women had found appealing. He tramped back, big gun swaying at his hip, the rowels of his Mexican spurs making a faint jingling sound.

"Leithbut isn't loco enough to sell Chainlink out from under me," he said, his voice rough. He seemed about to lift his big hands and shake the lie out of the doctor's corpulent frame, and knock off the hard hat Purcell wore on all occasions save when delivering babies or attending funerals.

Purcell told him how the stage driver had brought in the word not an hour before. Chainlink had been sold.

"You're a damned liar, Doc," Benbow said and strode into the hotel. The few men lounging in the lobby had overheard the exchange between Benbow and the doctor on the porch. Now they stood in various awkward poses, some of them smiling tensely at the son of the man who had kept a spurred boot in the face of West Texas for so long.

Benbow strode to the desk where a white-faced clerk was licking his lips. "Leithbut still got the same room?"

"He—he ain't here no more, Mr. Benbow."

Benbow rose up on the tips of his boot toes.

A faint scar above his right eye gave him a startled interrogative look at times.

"Where'd Leithbut go?" Benbow demanded.

"California, I hear."

Benbow turned and strode across the street and up a flight of stairs to offices above the West Texas Store. The office that Leithbut, dealer in land and cattle, had occupied for so long was empty. The furniture had been moved out.

Benbow stared at the empty office, then at the oilskin packet that contained his contract for beef next year. Offered only on the proviso that he be able to buy Chainlink back from Leithbut, who had foreclosed on him. And then borrow money from Leithbut to stock the ranch. The packing house would put up the money to buy back Chainlink, but not to buy cattle. That was Benbow's part of the deal. But he had been confident the money would be forthcoming from Leithbut. He had figured Leithbut was too scared to refuse. For the year since Leithbut had taken over Chainlink, Benbow knew the man had been living in fear of his life; and Clyde Benbow took pleasure in letting him wonder if and when he would find his grave. The cattle on Chainlink had been sold off and the ranch allowed to run down. All that Benbow had left were a few sections he called the "Little Place." He had had such high hopes of regaining control of Chainlink, but now—Leithbut not only had failed to loan him money to stock the ranch, he'd sold the land out from under him.

A silence fell over the Del Carmen House Bar when Benbow entered. "How long's Leithbut been gone?" Benbow demanded of the saloon's owner, Jim Penwade.

"He ain't been around for a few days, Clyde," Penwade said, and ran a nervous hand over his thin, center-parted hair. With an effort he pulled his gaze away from Benbow's furious face and set out a bottle and glass and poured a drink.

Benbow downed the whisky, feeling the warmth that only intensified his rage, and he thought darkly, *I guess Leithbut forgot I said I'd kill him if he sold.*

A thin man with a star pinned to his narrow chest came up from where some men were sitting amidst cards and chips of an interrupted stud game. Everybody in the place watched Sheriff Sam Enright look casually at Clyde Benbow, and lean an arm on the bar.

"Don't take Leithbut sellin' too much to heart, Clyde," the sheriff said. Enright was in his late forties, a man who had spent a lifetime in the saddle. He had a drink. His voice and his hand were steady. "Not hard like your daddy would have taken it. I won't stand for no killing over this, Clyde."

Benbow's lips curled. "Poppa made you a sheriff, Sam," he said while the room grew silent. "You were nothing but a twenty-dollar hand. But Poppa hung that badge on you." Benbow gave those in the room a slow arrogant smile, then put his eyes back on Enright's red face. "Funny that these boys keep electing you to office. I thought by this time they'd know you've got the guts of a mouse without the Chainlink crew riding behind you."

Sam Enright winced but he did not turn away. "Things are different around here, Clyde, since your poppa died. And your brother Tom's gone. We won't stand for a Benbow running this country."

"I hope you've got a tough stomach, Sam, because one day I'm going to make you eat that badge, pin and all."

Benbow was striding for the doorway when Enright's enraged voice reached him. "For one,

I'm damned glad Leithbut had the guts to sell to somebody else," the sheriff said.

Benbow turned and came back. As if realizing he might have gone too far, he forced a smile on his unwilling mouth. "Guess my tongue sort of ran away with me, Sam."

Enright refused to accept the forced apology. He looked around. "Any time you boys figure I'm not doing a good job, you can set me down come next election."

When the sheriff was gone a silence claimed the room for a moment. There was a clearing of throats and a shifting of feet. Some of those who were still awed by the power the Benbows once wielded, spoke their minds: "Sam oughta watch out talkin' up to you thataway, Clyde." "We sure are sorry about you losin' Chainlink." "I hope Leithbut gets cramps in his fingers from spendin' all that money in Frisco."

Benbow came back to the bar and Jim Penwade put out bottles and the house bought a drink. Benbow felt the whisky surge through him. It erased the tiredness in his big body and sharpened his mind. A name kept whipping through his consciousness. California. California.

"So Leithbut's gone to California," he said,

trying to speak casually, but he was mentally mapping out the various routes and modes of transportation Leithbut might take to get there. He bought a round of drinks.

"He was scared white," Penwade said, as he wrote down the drinks on the Benbow tab. If the Benbow fortunes didn't improve he might never be paid. But he didn't dare mention this possibility. Not with Clyde Benbow in his present mood. "Leithbut sold his desk and his chair to Doc Purcell. Closed up his office. Then he hires the Oakum brothers for bodyguards and went hightailin' it outa town."

"On the stage?" Benbow asked with apparent indifference.

"Saddle," Penwade said.

Benbow's eyes lighted. Saddle horses left tracks and he figured there was no trail he couldn't follow. But this was no time to go busting out. He'd round up Keller and Lawler and Macready and ride out tonight. Then at sunup they'd look for the trail—

He was aware that Penwade had been talking and now the saloonman's conversation began to penetrate.

". . . and George said he was looking for you," the saloonman was saying. "But I told him he better get outa town. Seein' as what you did to him last time."

Benbow's head jerked up and he studied the sallow face of the saloonman, whose hair was so heavily laden with sweet-smelling pomade that it drew the flies.

"George who?" Benbow demanded.

"George Wheat."

Benbow poured himself another drink. "Have I got to run him out again?"

"Never thought he'd soften down to a man, Clyde, like he done to you," Penwade said, and there was a vigorous nodding of heads in agreement. "Puttin' a bent nail in the end of a piece of rope and whippin' him bloody with it."

"He deserved it," Benbow said thinly. "I told him to stay away from my sister."

"Nobody but a Benbow could think of putting a bent nail in a piece of rope." It was Purcell, who had come in for his afternoon drink. Benbow wheeled and glared at him and the doctor added, "I mean it's the sort of thing you or your late poppa would do. But not your brother Tom. Tom Benbow was a gentleman and a gentle man."

"You mean, Doc," Benbow said, "that you

58

wish it was me who was dead instead of Tom. Be like you to claim I killed him."

"We all remember how Tom died," Purcell said. "He tried to take a gun away from a drink-crazy cowboy . . ."

"A fool trick."

". . . in order to save the lives of women and children in town for a Saturday outing. This boy shooting his gun, daring anybody to take him. And the sheriff out of town. And nobody but Tom having the guts to step up. And Tom getting shot dead for it."

"You know what happened to that cowhand," Benbow reminded the tense crowd. "I hung him personally."

"A fine accomplishment," Purcell pressed on. "Hanging a man who didn't know his own name. Too drunk to even walk." He stared at the whisky glass in his hand. "Sometimes I wonder why I drink this stuff." But he downed the drink, and refilled his glass.

Benbow glared at the doctor. Penwade, anxious to get the conversation back on safer grounds, said, "You fellas remember the night George Wheat took on them three bullwhackers from Santa Fe? They was big men, but George sure fixed 'em. I hear one of them boys died later."

"And another one in that outfit still can't walk, so I hear," a man put in.

"Just why'd you run George off Chainlink, Clyde?"

"I told you," Benbow said, and with an effort tore his gaze from Purcell's bland face. "Because he was loco about my sister. Followed her around like a hound dog after bear. I knew damn well if I didn't get rid of him—" His eyes swung back to Purcell. "I s'pose my gentleman brother would have said 'too bad' if that sand-brained giant pinned Lisa down in the dark somewhere. But I'd hang him, Doc. Like I did that cowhand that shot Tom."

"You're getting drunk, Clyde," the doctor said mildly. "You're also a vengeful man."

"Vengeful because I'd hang the man that ruined my sister?"

Purcell looked up from his second drink. "Too bad Maydelle Ashley never had a brother. Maybe you'd be the one with your neck tied to a tree limb."

In the awed silence Benbow's face lost color. But no one laughed. No face in the tense room

60

altered expression. Purcell finished his drink and walked out.

Benbow followed him to the hotel porch where the sun was warm against their faces. In the distance the Davis Mountains humped their backs against the horizon.

"Why're you pushing me today, Doc?" Benbow said through his teeth.

"Because I have a feeling a lot of mothers' sons are going to die. And I get sick at my stomach every time I think about it."

"One of these days you're going to put your tongue to my name once too often."

Purcell shrugged his fat shoulders. "I'm an old man and I don't care very much. But remember this, Clyde. You could kill any man in this town. Even the sheriff, maybe. And you might get away with it. But don't try it on me."

"You God or something?"

"I've delivered too many babies in this county, Clyde. I've also brought too many mothers' sons from the grave edge with their bones broken and their life pouring out through a bullet hole. They'd tear you to pieces, Clyde. Remember that."

"Don't be too sure, Doc."

"You're through here, Clyde. Why don't you get out?"

"I swore I'd own Chainlink again. And I will."

From the porch Benbow watched Purcell move along the walk toward his cottage beyond the feed store. He saw the doctor stop, talk with passersby. And Benbow thought, *I've never walked down this street and had a man say a pleasant word to me and mean it. I've never had a slap on the shoulder. Not with a friendly hand.*

But self-pity left him like a discarded coat when he saw his sister Lisa ride into town. Tired as he was, enraged at Leithbut's doublecross, his face still lighted at sight of her.

She saw him on the porch and rode up swiftly and dismounted and ran to him and hugged him. "Oh, Clyde, I just heard you were back."

He guessed from her stricken face that she knew Chainlink had been sold. But she had other news. Keller was dead. Shot by a man named Griff Jordan. Chainlink's new range boss.

Benbow gripped the porch railing in his big hands. "So we've got a backshooter to neighbor with," he said, and drew his .44 and lifted the hammer and let it down.

"Keller wasn't shot in the back."

"Nobody could kill Keller unless they came for him at the back."

Lisa shook her pale head. She told how she had witnessed the killing, how Jordan had let Keller get his gun loose and then shot him.

"I don't believe it," Benbow said in a low voice.

"It's true, Clyde." She drew him to a bench on the porch while she told him what had happened. How Keller had insisted on going back to Elvine's Store. She caught the big hands of this man who shared her name. "Clyde, let's not have any more shooting like there was when Poppa was alive."

"There was no shooting when Tom was ramrodding Chainlink," he said thinly.

"Tom tried to get along with people, Clyde. You don't. You antagonize—"

"You wish it was me dead, not Tom?"

"No, Clyde." She shook her head, her eyes closed. "It was God's will that Tom died. I don't know why he was taken. We can't understand these things." She turned on the bench, her eyes pleading. "Clyde, don't try to get even for Keller."

Clyde Benbow sat looking at her, studying the oval face, the small perfect nose, the mouth full and wide, the chin that showed her strength and her occasional stubbornness.

"I've missed you, Lisa," he said quietly. "Two months I've been gone. And then to come home to this."

"Clyde, let's go away. We can sell the 'Little Place.'"

"We'll own Chainlink again."

"It's gone now, Clyde. Nothing will bring it back."

He was staring at the distant mountains. "I wanted to use a gun and take Chainlink from Leithbut. But you begged me to go slow. To wait and see if we couldn't raise the money."

"It was the right way."

"Oh, no. Don't use a gun on Leithbut. Honest Leithbut, who gave his word he'd never sell to another man as long as there was a chance I could raise the money."

She stared at the ugly twist of his mouth and guessed his thoughts. "A man breaks his word. Is it right to kill him?"

"I've got to have Chainlink. I've got to."

"But it's been sold. Can't you understand that?" She put a hand on his arm. "Besides, Chainlink didn't bring us much happiness. Even when we were children."

It brought a flicker of a smile across his lips. "I remember the night you were born, Lisa. You howled for hours."

"And Momma died that night." Lisa looked away. "Clyde, please try to remember how our mother was. She was a gentle person like Tom."

His lips curled and he stared bitterly at those passing on the walks below. And the moment of gentleness with Lisa became washed in the hard core of his determination to regain possession of Chainlink. It didn't matter how he accomplished this. It didn't matter at all. Chainlink was his life. It was the only thing he wanted. The only thing that made any difference whether he lived or died. And then Lisa's calm voice was reaching him and he knew there was one other thing that mattered. Lisa mattered.

". . . I don't know what George could want back here in Texas. But I saw him at Elvine's Store."

Benbow gave her a tight smile. "I heard he was back. George won't bother you—"

"Don't drive him out like you did before. That was horrible, Clyde. It's a wonder he didn't try to kill you."

"He might try if it wasn't for you. He knows you'd hate him for it. '

"He didn't bother me when he was here before, Clyde. I tried to tell you that he was just like a big shaggy dog following me around. He was very gentle with me, Clyde. A gentleman—"

Benbow sprang to his feet, the muscles taut along his jaws. "I've had enough gentleness for one day, Lisa," he said stiffly. "You go on home. I've got some things to do."

He hurried her away, because from the slot running between the hotel and the next establishment, with its sign: *J. Edelmann, Gunsmith*, he saw the towering George Wheat. And Wheat was shaking his head at Lisa's back and then putting a finger across his lips to signify silence.

When Lisa was gone, Clyde Benbow came off the porch. "I ran you out once. You back for more of the same?"

"I was in Tucson. I heard somebody talkin'

about the Benbows. It was Major Clay that bought Chainlink. I signed on and trailed back here with his outfit."

"That the reason you came back? Because you like the gent that bought me out?"

"I wrote you a letter, but Lisa opened it."

"You came back because you're in love with my sister."

Wheat turned red. He leaned close and whispered, "I know where Leithbut's gone."

"To California."

Wheat shook his head. "Mexico. I know which road he's takin'."

5

GRIFF JORDAN carried the major into one of the back bedrooms of the sprawling mud-walled house at Chainlink. Once again he tried as he had many times during the long ride from Elvine's Store, to get him to talk. But the major pretended he was too badly injured to discuss the matter of why he had found it necessary to get drunk the moment Griff's back was turned.

Leaving Ed Damon to see that the herd was spread out over the Chainlink domain, he saddled a fresh horse and headed for Del Carmen. It was more practical to take the major to the doctor's in town and let him stay there until he recovered from the beating. But in that event the major would be vulnerable if Benbow decided to follow up on the grim business started by Keller.

It was dark when he reached the outskirts of Del Carmen with its windows aglow with lamplight, the haze of charcoal fires hanging in a blue wave above the 'dobe and frame buildings.

Reining in at the curb Griff asked a man sweeping the steps of the West Texas Store where he might find a doctor. The man said Doc Purcell was playing cards at the Del Carmen House.

The first thing Griff saw upon entering the saloon was a flag over the backbar. The stars and bars of the Confederacy. He felt a tautness in his throat and turned away to order himself a drink. Now was the test, he told himself. He was back among his fellow Texans. Would there be someone in the dozen or so drinkers at the bar who would remember Bullhide Jordan and his two sons from down in the brush country?

But no one spoke to him. He listened to the drift of talk, learning that Clyde Benbow had returned from Kansas that day and was some "het up on account of Leithbut sellin' him out." The consensus of opinion seemed to be that it would be a welcome day when Clyde Benbow quit the Del Carmen country for good.

After making inquiries Griff found Purcell in a private card room. The plump doctor, wearing his hard hat, leaned back in a chair when Griff told him there'd been a beating, that a man was hurt.

The other players exchanged glances when

they learned the beaten man was the new owner of Chainlink.

"Looks like Benbow's started to work already," Purcell grunted.

He hurried off to the stable to get his buggy, leaving Griff on the porch. Griff remembered then that one of his missions in town was to bring Maydelle Ashley back to Chainlink. In the moments when the major was irrational from the whisky and his injuries, he kept calling for his niece. He had meant to get the girl's address from the doctor.

When he saw a woman approaching along the walk, Griff stepped down and tipped his hat and asked where he might find Maydelle Ashley. With a snort of disgust, the woman hurried along the walk, her nose in the air.

Griff heard a titter behind him and turned to see an old man sitting on a loafer's bench, smoking a pipe. "You'll find Maydelle at the end of Rojo Street. Big two-story house." He pointed with his pipe stem toward the south end of town.

Giving the old man a brief nod, Griff got his horse and rode south. He came to a shed with a sign and an arrow that said Rojo Street. He continued down a dark tree-lined street. At the end of the street he could see lamplight at curtained windows.

Griff left his horse beside two other saddlers and climbed the steps to the porch of an unpainted frame house. He knocked on a heavy plank door.

In a moment it opened and a girl with long black hair put her head out and said, "Come on in, honey. You don't have to knock."

"You Maydelle Ashley?"

The girl, holding the door wide, looked him over. "She'll be down directly. You come in the parlor and set."

But Griff stood rigid, aware of disgust and anger and a feeling that the major's grand dream was suddenly showing wide cracks in its masonry.

Two cowhands crossed the parlor, said something to the black-haired girl and went down the steps, putting on their hats.

Griff wheeled and followed them and the door slammed shut behind him. The two cowhands were already in the saddle, firing up cigars. One of them said, "Can't be choosy. Hell, there ain't another fancy house like this in two hundred miles."

Griff said nothing. He reined away and went

back uptown. He felt some of the major's sickness creeping in on him and he wanted to get drunk. Because he knew the town a little better now, he sent his roan across a weed-grown lot and so came up behind a small brick building with barred windows.

There was quite a crowd gathered and in a flare of light from the open doorway he could see a body lying on the walk. And he saw Lisa Benbow, a shawl over her head, wearing a blue dress, talking to a man with a star on his shirt.

Suddenly her eyes lifted and she saw Griff in the saddle at the far edge of the lamplight. "That's the one, Sam," she said.

Sam Enright turned and the crowd stirred. "You Griff Jordan?"

Griff swung down, his nerves taut. From the way the girl called the sheriff by his first name, it could mean he was a Benbow sheriff. Then anything could happen. But he grimly resolved, as he had in the past, that he would let nothing spoil this deal for him. Not a Benbow or a Benbow sheriff or Maydelle Ashley.

"Miss Benbow says you shot Keller in self-defense," the man with the badge said.

Griff nodded and his eyes sought Lisa's and for a moment they looked at each other, their faces stilled. Then Lisa turned and said, "You won't need me, Sam," and walked off into the darkness.

Sam Enright introduced himself and passed over a cigar to Griff. "Macready and Lawler brung the body in." Enright broke a matchhead on his bootsole and lit Griff's cigar. In the flare of light the sheriff's eyes studied the face of this Chainlink ramrod-partner. "To beat Keller you must be good, Jordan."

Griff said, "A man learns to fight for his life or he doesn't stay alive very long."

The sheriff nodded, and dropped the match. He turned to some men in the crowd and said, "Boys, take Keller down to the shed, will you?"

When the body was being carried away, Enright called Griff into the jail office and offered him a chair. Griff sank down, realizing only now how tired he was.

"I like Major Clay," Enright said, and put a haunch on the edge of a rolltop desk. On the wall was a gunrack and a feed company calendar. "He was down here a few months back lookin' around. Fine man. Doubly welcome because he's a CSA man."

Griff removed the cigar from his mouth and stared at it a moment, wondering if the sheriff would say any more about the major's previous visit. Such as: "Too bad his niece didn't turn out so well." But no mention of Maydelle Ashley.

Now the sheriff was talking about the Benbows and how Clyde was obsessed with the idea of again owning Chainlink. "Lisa told me how the major got beat up by Keller. I don't think Clyde had anything to do with it because he wasn't back yet. But you watch out for Clyde. He's a tough one."

"I won't run from him," Griff said. "By the way, is he in town?"

"I hear he rode out with George Wheat."

Griff got up and said as long as the matter of Keller's death seemed to be settled he guessed he should be getting back to the ranch.

At the door he turned and said, "We'll have quite a crew out at Chainlink before we're through. I guess you have the usual cowtown diversions for the hands. Liquor and everything else."

"You mean girls?" The sheriff looked grim. "Yeah. A two-story house at the end of Rojo Street. Run by Maydelle Ashley."

"Oh, yes, I remember hearing her name. Raised around here, wasn't she?"

74

"Yep."

"Didn't she have any kin to keep her straight?" Griff asked mildly.

"Her father was shot when she was just a baby, and her mother died soon after. But that was before my time. She was brought up by the Goodriches over on Median Creek."

The sheriff followed Griff to the door and said, "Don't think downing Keller gives you a killing license here, Jordan. I got a rope that'll fit any man's neck."

"Tell that to Benbow. But if he tries to take back Chainlink by force, you won't need that rope."

When Griff rode the eight miles to Chainlink, Ed Damon, holding a lantern, met him in the yard. Purcell's buggy team was tied to the porch rail. Damon seemed surprised that Griff hadn't brought out the major's niece.

"He's been askin' for her," the segundo said.

Griff swung down and told Damon what he had learned about Maydelle Ashley. When he had finished Damon gave a low whistle. "If he learns this it might do him in." Damon's one eye looked grim. "Bein' beat up and all the way he is."

"I don't know for sure, but I've got a hunch

he already knows about her. That's why he's been drinking so much." Griff swore and looked at the lighted squares of windows in the mud-walled house. He opened a big hand, closed it slowly. "I thought I had a good chunk of the world right here, Ed. Now I don't know."

"You reckon this gal can bust the spokes outa the wheel and ruin things for you and the major?"

Griff shrugged. "Keep this under your hat, Ed."

The doctor came out of the house then, wearing his hard hat, carrying his bag. Griff walked over and asked if the major's injuries were serious. Purcell said there were no punctured lungs from broken ribs. Something to be thankful for.

Griff followed him to the buggy. "You heard the major raving about his niece?"

Purcell put his black bag on the floorboards. "He's feverish. A man says a lot of things under those conditions." Then he added, "No use fooling you, Jordan. Yes, he mentioned Maydelle Ashley."

"And you know about her, Doc."

"Do you?"

Griff told about asking the woman on the street where he might find Maydelle Ashley. "She hurried away as if I'd had the plague."

The doctor made a clucking sound. "Maydelle is a foolish woman," the doctor said. "Some call her a sinful one."

"And what do you call her, Doc?"

"A man once said something about throwing the first stone if you're without sin. Me, I only deal with human beings, with sin or without."

"I think I'm going to like you, Doc."

"Maybe we'll have a long friendship. I hope so." Purcell put a hand on Griff's arm. "We don't get many men like you and the major in these parts. I'd enjoy discussing the affairs of the world with you both some night over a bottle of brandy at my place."

"I'll look forward to it."

"By the way, keep the major away from whisky."

"It's enough to make a man want to drown himself in the stuff. Knowing your own kin is a—" Griff didn't finish it.

"Drinking like that is retreat. No problem can be solved unless you advance."

"That sounds like army talk, Doc."

"I served with Jackson."

Griff instantly felt ice along his spine and cursed himself for mentioning the war. Now Purcell was peering at him in the darkness, waiting. In these times a man intending to live in a territory formerly governed by the CSA stated his own war record when such an opening was made by another. And Purcell was still waiting.

"I understand you saved the major's life in the war," Purcell said finally. "Were you one of his officers?"

Griff was untying the doctor's team. "Want me to ride to town with you, Doc?"

"I'll manage."

"Might be Comanches out."

"Not for a long time. Besides, they wouldn't get much." Purcell removed his hard hat to reveal a shiny bald head.

Then, with a dry laugh, he put on the hat and climbed into the buggy and picked up the reins. "That long friendship between us that we spoke of. Let's see it thrive. And in order to do that—so it isn't cut off abruptly—keep away from Clyde Benbow if you can. If you can't, you'll have to kill him."

Griff said nothing. He stood rigid, his face pale, in a shaft of lamplight fanning out from the front windows of the house. And irrelevantly his thoughts swung suddenly from the trap he had set for himself with the doctor and went to something more pleasant. He thought of the countless times Lisa Benbow had crossed this very porch, maybe tended flowers she had planted around the house. Lisa growing up here, riding her first horse here—

Purcell said, "Forget my bringing up the war. It was none of my business who you fought with or against. But you talk Texian and I thought—"

"I was born down in the brush country."

"Brush country, eh? I recollect a Jordan down there years ago. They called him Bullhide Jordan because he got rich before the war, selling hides. Any kin?"

Still Griff did not speak.

Purcell gave a dry laugh. "I'm getting old. When a man asks too many questions in country like this it shows he's got the breath of the grave blowing up his trousers leg. Good luck, Jordan. I'll be looking forward to our talk."

Griff said, "I'd appreciate it if you don't spread it around that the major is the Ashley woman's uncle. Although they'll know it soon enough, I suppose."

"If I set my mind to it I can keep my mouth shut."

He turned and waved at Griff and was about to lift the reins. And Griff, starting to move away from the porch, heard a thrashing of air just under his left armpit and a solid thunking sound in the mud wall behind him. In the distance a red eye winked. Griff shouted to Purcell to get away. But the doctor's team, spooked by the firing and the yell, lunged forward and dragged the buggy on two wheels around a corner of the house and into the darkness.

The moment he shouted, Griff was diving headfirst for the shadows, trying to get out of the circle of lamplight from the windows. The thunking sound came again and another red eye. And another. The ground jarred under him and as he reached for his gun a bullet hit the hard pan and went wheeling with a ghastly screech toward the stars.

As Griff reached shadows and came up with his gun he heard only the sounds of two horses being put to a hard run beyond the corral. He emptied his gun, knowing the range was too long. The bunkhouse door was open and the men piled out, led by Ed Damon. There was much shouting and milling around. The horses in the corral were snorting, kicking up their heels.

Swiftly Griff reloaded his gun and raced for the corral where saddled horses were kept ready for instant riding. As Ed Damon shouted questions, Griff tightened a cinch and swung aboard.

Jerking free a booted rifle, he spurred off. There were the sounds of two horses out there, fading fast. And there was no moon. Just let me get my sights on one of them, he thought. Just one. The dirty bushwhackers.

But in the darkness he lost the sound of them. If he only had Indian blood in his veins he could have trailed them by the scent of dust left by their racing mounts.

But he was no Indian. He was just a man who was trying desperately at the tag end of his youth to capitalize on the golden chance offered by a drunken ex-major with a niece who would sell herself quicker than a man would sell his saddle.

He turned back for the house and met Damon and the crew saddled up and waving rifles and shouting. Griff told them it was no use trying to trail in the dark. There were questions hammered at Griff, but he was too enraged to answer.

He rode back across the yard and saw Purcell in his buggy. Doc said, "This team must've smelled skunk. They took off like they were shot from Johnny Reb cannon. Did you get hit, Jordan?"

"No." Griff swung down, seeing the scuffed places on the ground where the bullets had grooved the dust. "It was damned close. If I hadn't moved just then." Cold sweat broke out on his back.

"You think Benbow is starting to work by the dark of the moon?" Purcell said.

"Two horses out there," Griff said, staring off into the darkness. "That means two men. The sheriff said Benbow and George Wheat rode out of town together tonight."

"That's a strange combination," Purcell murmured. "They were enemies once."

"Or it might be Macready and Lawler, getting back for what I did to their friend Keller." Doc hadn't heard of this and Griff had to give all the details.

"Whoever was out there in the dark," the

doctor said gravely, "intended to kill you. No mistake about that."

"I'll know better than to have a lamp at my back again."

"Here's a suggestion," Purcell said. "Before this thing goes any deeper ride over and have a talk with Lisa Benbow at the 'Little Place.' It's about ten miles east of here. She's a sensible girl. And she's the only human on this earth who could talk to Clyde. Try it, Jordan."

He drove off and Griff went into the house and to the room the major occupied. The major lay in a big double bed, his swollen eyes closed.

"What was the shooting about, Griff?" The major's voice sounded strange and far away.

Griff told him. The major said nothing. Griff stood at the foot of the bed for a long moment and he had a strange feeling as if he could catch a woman's scent. And then he wondered, with his pulse quickening, if this might not be the room Lisa Benbow had occupied for so long. Lying on that bed as the major was now lying —He closed his eyes, and thought, I'll give it one chance. I'll take Doc's suggestion and have a talk with her. But if she can't hold her brother in then a lot of dying is due for this end of Texas.

"Milo," Griff said, coming around the foot of the bed and peering down at the slightly-built figure under the blankets. "I know about your niece. It's all right, Milo. I understand why you've been drinking. We'll work it out. But just confide in me after this. After all, we're partners."

But the major must have drifted off to sleep, for he made no reply.

Griff tiptoed out and went to his own bedroom.

After a sleepless night he dressed at dawn and went out to look for sign. Beyond the corral he saw several gleaming brass shells, and the tracks of two men and their horses. The tracks led east. The "Little Place" Doc spoke of was over that way.

In that moment, with the rising sun in his eyes, he felt caught up in a whirlpool and knew that Lisa Benbow was struggling just as hard as he against the strong pull of the current.

6

THREE days later Clyde Benbow and George Wheat returned to Del Carmen. On their way out to the "Little Place" they ran into Mark Goodrich. Old man Goodrich had ranched over east since right after the Mexican War. Benbow was in a high good humor and told Goodrich that he wanted to buy a prize bull the rancher had for sale.

Goodrich, a shrewd, sun-baked little man, scratched his gray thatch and gave Benbow a sidelong glance. "That bull is worth ten thousand, but I'll take six."

"Surprised you'd sell to me, Mark," Benbow said with a grin.

"Right now I'd have to sell to Satan himself if he was a buyer. I need money." Goodrich added, "I'll want cash for that bull, Clyde."

"And you'll get cash," Benbow said easily. "I got money coming from Chicago."

"You marry a rich Yankee gal while you was north?"

"I got me a fancy beef contract. From one

of those big Chicago packing houses. They're shipping me a wagonload of cash"—and seeing George Wheat's sudden stiffening in the saddle beyond Goodrich's shoulder, Clyde Benbow added, "I mean a whole box full of cash money."

Goodrich looked skeptical. "A Yank packing house won't loan money unless a man's got beef on the hoof. You got nothin' but the 'Little Place.' You couldn't graze enough beef on that to raise a spoonful of manure dust in a high wind."

"I'm buyin' me a herd with the money they're sending," Benbow said, his voice confident. "I'm looking long-range, Mark. I want that bull of yours to breed up my stuff."

"Now if you still had Chainlink, I'd say you might be talkin' straight, but—"

"Might surprise some folks around here," Benbow said, his mouth suddenly tight, "if I bought Chainlink back."

"You'll never see that much money, Clyde."

"You might be awful wrong, Mark. Awful wrong."

"From what I hear, Major Clay won't sell, no matter what."

"Maybe he'll get laughed outa the country, Mark. Ever think of that?"

"Laughed out? Why so?"

"He's uncle to Maydelle Ashley."

Goodrich went white. "I don't believe it."

"Ask George Wheat." Benbow turned to the giant in the saddle of a Morgan horse big enough to carry his weight. "When you was hired on in Tucson you recollect the major talking about his niece, don't you?"

"It's Maydelle Ashley, all right," Wheat said.

Goodrich sat his saddle, trembling. "By God, Clyde, I wish I had the guts to blow you outa your boots. Whatever that girl done is on account of you."

"Lot of wind over the fence since then," Benbow said curtly. "I'll send Macready and Lawler over for that bull."

Benbow and Wheat rode off, leaving Goodrich in his impotent fury. When Benbow sighted the two-room shack he now called home, his stomach turned. This place had once been a line camp. He resolved then and there to better Lisa's living conditions. There was a house for sale in town. He'd buy it for her.

As they rode in, Benbow told Wheat to go to the bunkhouse, which was little more than a lean-to against the barn, and take Keller's bunk. Keller wouldn't be needing it.

Then Lisa came around the corner of the house, shading her eyes against the sun to see who had ridden in. She wore a faded blue dress that she kept starched and clean and her hair, slicked back, caught the sunlight.

George Wheat reined in and sat staring. "By damn, Clyde, her hair shines like gold that's just come from the mint."

Benbow jerked around in the saddle. "You better forget about what looks like gold that just came from the mint."

"Yeah? How about you tellin' Goodrich about a wagonload of money—"

"You better shut up, George," Benbow said softly. "I've got another bent nail I can put in the end of a rope."

"Not now you won't." George Wheat folded his big hands over the saddle horn. "We're in it together. Up to our necks."

Benbow bit back an oath, seeing Lisa coming across the yard with her long-legged stride. The breeze pressed her dress flat against her and, noticing this, she seemed embarrassed. She slowed and turned sideways and with her fingers plucked the garment away from her body.

"Howdy, Miss Benbow," George Wheat said in an awed voice, and slid to the ground. He removed his hat, and his thick neck reddened, the color spreading around his ears and across the planes of his face.

Lisa gave the big man a brief nod, then drew Clyde aside. "Clyde, we have company. It's a chance for peace, and I want you to take it."

Benbow frowned but decided to humor Lisa. After all he was in high spirits. He jerked his head at Wheat, who led the two saddlers across the yard. Then with his arm about Lisa's waist, Clyde Benbow walked the girl toward the house.

"Why have you brought George Wheat back here?" Lisa demanded. "And where have you been for the past few days?"

He ignored her questions. "Won't hurt to give Wheat a smile once in a while. Now what's this about peace?"

But he didn't really listen to Lisa. He was thinking of the strangers living in the house at Chainlink. The house where Lisa was born. The house where he had lived for most of his life.

As they swung around a corner of the house Benbow slowed when for the first time he saw a horse tied off in the shade and a man leaning against the 'dobe wall.

"Who's that?" he demanded under his breath.

She told him it was Griff Jordan. "He wants to be neighborly, Clyde—"

"He kills one of my men and he wants to be neighborly." He glanced back over his shoulder, wondering if Macready and Lawler were in the bunkhouse. But he saw only Wheat, lugging his gear into the bunkhouse. Not that he needed help, he told himself. But he was remembering how fast this Jordan must be to down a slick like Keller.

"Two men tried to kill Jordan the other night," Lisa said under her breath, and looked up, as if trying to read Benbow's face. "It might have been you and George Wheat. Or did you tell Macready and Lawler to do it?"

"I've been away on business," he snapped. Jordan was watching their approach. "I got nothing to say about Macready and Lawler. They do what they please. Besides, Jordan's probably making up the story to get your sympathy."

"Doc Purcell was there when it happened. He told me about it the next day."

Lisa introduced the two men and they regarded each other warily. Benbow didn't want to offer his hand but Lisa looked so damned beautiful and sincere and wanting peace that he finally put it out.

"Howdy, Jordan," he said, and tried mightily to keep his voice level. For Lisa's sake.

Jordan nodded a greeting, but didn't say anything. Benbow had the feeling that those quick brown eyes were studying him as he had never been studied before. And all at once he felt naked and ill-at-ease and wondering if those eyes were going deep into his brain and reading there all the ugliness of the past days.

Jordan was talking about the attempted ambush the other night. "I followed their trail come sunup, but lost it down near the river. I'm not accusing you, Benbow; I'm just stating facts. My men have orders to run trespassers off Chainlink or shoot them."

Benbow's mouth went white. *You, giving orders on Chainlink, the ranch I should own!*

Lisa must have seen the beginnings of a storm in Benbow's eyes, for she said, "Please, Clyde. Hear him out."

"I'm willing to forget everything, Benbow," Griff Jordan said. "The beating of my partner, Major Clay, and the attempt on my life. I'd rather live in peace in this country. And your sister agrees that this is the only way."

"Then talk your major into selling back Chainlink. I'll pay as much as he did. Or almost. A note for the rest."

"You find a gold mine?" Jordan said. "I heard you were broke."

"Fortunes change," Benbow said easily.

"The major won't sell his share and I won't sell mine."

"And just how do you earn your share of a ranch that size? By having a faster gun than the next man?"

"That's my business," Jordan said quietly. "I know how much you counted on owning Chainlink again. But one man's fortune is another man's bad luck. Now I was thinking maybe we could lease some of your sections for graze. I'd consider it as a partial payment for your disappointment in not getting Chainlink—"

A sharp triumph surged through Benbow. *He's trying to crawl*, he thought. *He doesn't want to fight. He wants the easy way. Like Tom . . .*

"Couldn't accept your offer," Benbow said, a stiff smile on his lips.

Lisa had been regarding Clyde Benbow narrowly. "We could use the money, Clyde."

"We'll need the land for our own cattle."

"But we have none," she said.

"We're buying cattle," Benbow said, and caught a speculative look in Jordan's eyes. Benbow lost his feeling of triumph.

Trying to sound convincing, for Lisa's sake again, he told about the wonderful deal with the Chicago packing house. "In fact, I'll have to lease more range myself. Goodrich has about forty sections he's not using. Since his wife died, he's had no stomach for ranching—"

Benbow's voice trailed off; the brown eyes were studying him, weighing him again. Suddenly the temper he had held on tight reins because of Lisa broke loose.

"One thing," he said, his voice thin and ugly, "if you and the major go broke at Chainlink, he can get a job working the front door at Maydelle Ashley's place. Kinfolks oughta stick together—"

He saw the flame in Jordan's eyes, and

reached for his gun, knowing he could shoot the other man to pieces.

Before he had the gunsight clear of holster leather Jordan's big arm flashed out and pinned Benbow against the house wall. The impact was so violent that the gun was knocked from Benbow's hand and lay gleaming in the dust.

As the two men glared at each other, Lisa put her hands over her mouth and said, "Please, please, please—"

Her voice broke the tension, and Jordan stepped back, his lips pale. "Don't ever say a thing like that again, Benbow. I mean it."

Benbow stepped away from the house wall, looked at his gun on the ground but didn't pick it up. "Wait'll everybody knows that the major's niece is Maydelle Ashley. You'll hear 'em laugh clean to Austin."

"I don't advise you making a joke of it," Jordan said. Then he tipped his hat to Lisa. "I'm hoping you can talk some sense into your brother."

He got his horse and rode out and when his dust was only a faint haze Lisa's body lost its rigidity and she turned on Benbow and said, "Oh, damn you, Clyde. Damn you! Why

94

couldn't you for once have done the decent thing!"

She whirled for the house and went in, slamming the door. Benbow stood for a moment, looking at George Wheat, who had come out of the bunkhouse to see who had ridden out. He would tell Wheat that Jordan said some insulting things to Lisa. But he'd tell him to settle the matter in town. He wanted everybody to watch it.

Benbow went into the house and for a long moment stood outside Lisa's room, listening to her sobs. He closed his eyes. To live in the same house with her. To hear the rustle of her clothing at night. To hear her come to the door, wearing the long nightdress, her hair in braids, and say, *"I want to leave the door open tonight, Clyde, for some air. It's stifling. Do you mind?"*

"No, I don't mind."

God—not mind? He'd lie there and ache and toss.

And then the days when he filled the big wooden tub for her in the kitchen and then went outside and rolled and smoked cigarettes and then came in and saw the marks left by her wet feet on the floor and smelled the woman-fresh sweet smell of water he emptied into the yard . . .

Living here like they were brother and sister. The day he took her by the hand and walked with her again into the house at Chainlink, he would tell her. Tell her that whatever had been done, good or bad, the ugly parts, the killings. All done for her. *Lisa, I love you.*

That day he'd tell her the truth. He'd tell her where he came from. Not from the womb of the woman who had given her birth. Not from the seed of Poppa. No. From God alone knew where. From the bullrushes, maybe, like Moses. Along the river where maybe some smuggler's woman had thrown him out to die. And the old man had been down along the river that day, hearing a calf bawl and thinking it mired down in the mud. Cussing his Texas Benbow heart out because he might lose a cow. And hearing a wail, not made by a cow but made by a two-year-old boy. And the old man putting a dirty finger into a small mouth, and small teeth biting hard. And the old man looking at the torn skin and shouting: "Tough, by damn. Boot tough. Sonny, you're comin' home with me."

And Mrs. Benbow with her starched aprons

and smelling of spice and weeping, with her own son held tight against her, screaming, "Take him out of here! I won't have my Tom grow up with the likes of him!"

"He'll grow up! He'll be a Benbow! And if you ever say he ain't mine—ain't *ours*, I'll—" The old man showed her the torn finger and Tom said, "I'd like a brother, Momma. I really would," the first kind word Clyde Benbow had from the boy he grew to call his brother. And later Lisa was born.

Now Clyde Benbow knocked softly on the door, then opened it. Lisa lay face down across her bed, her petticoats peeled back like the white foam waves the wind sometimes churned up along the river.

He went to the bed and sat down and put a hand on her back and said, "I'm sorry, Lisa. But someday you'll understand."

7

FOR the next few days Griff worked from first light to last, searching out the best graze on Chainlink, spotting small bunches of cattle at various points where they could find grass and water. The days when he was at headquarters he had no communication with the major at all. Clay seemed to be in a stupor and Griff knew he was paying one of the hands to bring him whisky. At first Griff was angered, then he thought, *What the hell. It's the major's money. If he wants to buy his own shroud how can I stop him?*

The one-eyed Ed Damon had also noticed the major's lack of response. The major never joined the men in the big kitchen at mealtime. He just lay in his bedroom, his face turned toward the wall.

"I've got an idea he blames himself for what happened to his niece," Griff said one day.

Two days later Griff returned from a swing toward the border, trying to fix in his mind the boundaries of Chainlink. He found a pair of matched black horses in the corral and asked Damon about them. The major made arrangements to buy the horses when he was in Texas before, Damon said. He bought the horses from a rancher named Goodrich over on Median Creek.

"The major paid a lot more'n them hosses is worth," Damon said. "And I told him so when he sent me over to pick 'em up. But he wouldn't listen."

"He needs that team of fancy steppers," Griff said tiredly, "like I need double heels on my boots."

That evening after supper he made another attempt to talk to the major about Maydelle Ashley. But the major refused to discuss it. Griff, looking at the face that now had partially healed from the brutal beating, knew the major was drunk as Christmas Eve.

Knowing he had to reach a decision and soon, Griff paced the yard in the darkness, careful to keep out of the glow of houselights. He intended to give no one else a chance to skylight him.

Perhaps if Maydelle Ashley was eliminated as a source of irritation and disgrace, the major would return to normal. There were many things that needed discussing. They had to decide whether to drive to Kansas or let the herd grow for a year. There was the matter of bills due at the stores in Del Carmen.

Griff went to his room and from behind a loose brick, removed a leather sack of gold coins. It was a thousand dollars that the major had paid him when they signed their contract in Virginia City last year. Putting the sack in his pocket, he went out and saddled a fresh horse.

At the Del Carmen House he drank his whisky and listened to the talk. Nobody mentioned the fact that the major was kin to Maydelle Ashley, but several men inquired after the major's health.

"Benbow's out to cut you under, Jordan," one of them said. "He paid cash for a bull from Mark Goodrich. I hear he's buyin' cattle, too."

Griff had another drink, frowning into the smoky darkness above the overhead reflectors. "Seems like Benbow got unbroke all of a sudden," he commented.

"I hope you and the major run him clean to Chihuahua," the man said.

Every time Griff decided to do what he had come to town for, he backed down. He drank and sat in a card game and won a little money. He looked up once and saw Macready and Lawler watching him in the backbar mirror. After a time they drifted out.

He decided to get a room at the hotel. He didn't want to have to fight off those two back-shooters on a dark trail tonight.

In his hotel room Griff lay in the darkness, unable to sleep. He cursed the major's weakness. Clay wasn't the first man who had to face up to something as jarring to his pride as a wayward niece. What the hell was the matter with the man?

Early in the morning he got his horse from where he had left it at the stable and rode to the end of Rojo Street.

When he knocked on the front door of the big two-story structure, there was no response. He went around in back and saw a girl sitting on a three-legged stool before a tub of water being heated over a fire ring. She was running a bar of yellow soap through her wet hair. When she heard his step, she looked up, but showed no embarrassment because her dress hung down to her waist and her upper body was only covered by some thin undergarment.

"Maydelle Ashley?" he asked.

"It ain't noon yet. We don't open till noon. Yeah, I'm Maydelle. You're new around here."

She went on with the washing of her hair while he said, "I'm here on business," and she gave a short laugh and replied, "Why else would you come here, mister?"

She looked him over, parting her thick wet hair away from her eyes. Here was obviously a man who appealed to a woman. Not good-looking, maybe. But big and powerfully built and with a sort of subdued explosive quality behind his brown eyes. "I'm sorry you catched me like this," she said, and gave him a smile.

He sank down on his heels. "I'm asking a favor and I'm willing to pay."

The laugh again, bubbling from her red mouth. "I should hope you're willin' to pay."

"A thousand dollars," he said, and drew from his pocket a leather sack and tossed it at her. She looked at it lying on the ground at her feet. Water dripped from the ends of her hair, staining the leather sack.

The good humor fled her face, destroying its prettiness. Now the eyes were shrewd and hard and a little frightened. "Who sent you, mister? Clyde?"

"Clyde Benbow?"

"He's throwin' money around like Saturday night," she said scornfully. "Bought a house in town for his sister. Buyin' cattle. Buyin' a prize bull. Maybe he figures to buy me outa this country."

"Why should Benbow want to do that?"

"Never mind." With a wide sweeping motion she piled her wet hair on top of her head. "Why for a thousand dollars? Why?"

He told her about Major Clay. "Surely you've known about him."

"Sure. Some old drunk with gold in his teeth, claimin' I'm kin to him. I ain't got no kin, mister. I got nobody but Maydelle Ashley."

"How about Clyde Benbow?"

"That son of a bitch," she said. Her eyes filled with tears and she was busy retrieving the bar of soap from the tub of hot water.

"Clyde Benbow started you like this?" Griff said, and waved a hand at the big house.

She flashed him an angry look. "Ain't they told you about me, mister? Nobody started me in nothin'." She stood up, her lips trembling. "Now you get outa here."

"Your Uncle Milo is a sick man, Maydelle. Sick physically and mentally."

"I seen that soft-talkin' bastard around town

103

when he was here before he bought Chainlink. If he's kin why didn't he speak up then?"

"He was ashamed to."

The tears came then. "Shame? Then he ain't kin of mine. My kin got no shame!" She looked away at the distant hills, at the people hurrying along the walks at the other end of Rojo Street. The good end. "I ain't ashamed of what I am. I don't like it none, maybe. But I ain't ashamed. I'm alone in this world. I got no Uncle Milo."

"Milo Clay was your mother's brother. Don't you remember him at all?" Griff was beginning to wonder. Was the major's mind so saturated with whisky that he only thought he had a niece?

"My mother had one brother. His name was Sam Kinsfather. He was no good. He was kilt in the war."

"Do you remember him at all?"

"I seen him only once. The day it happened. I was three, maybe four. I don't rightly remember. But I don't want to remember him." Her voice rose. "I don't want to remember him at all."

"What did he do that was so terrible?"

"He didn't like my father. He follered us

here. And he killed Poppa. Shot him dead. Momma told me. She died three years later." She wiped her nose on her bare forearm. "I was brung up by a family named Goodrich over on Median Crick."

Griff could hear the steady drumming of his pulse. He was remembering the team of matched blacks that the major had bought from a man named Goodrich. Paying more, much more, than the horses were worth. Not going over there himself but sending Ed Damon.

Griff picked up the money sack and put it in her hands. "Go to Austin or San Antone, maybe. Close this place up. Stay three months or six. When the money runs out write me general delivery. The name is Griff Jordan. When you come back things will be different."

He rode out before she could say anything.

But he sensed she wouldn't go. Not if she ran true to type. She'd laugh about the thousand dollars in some shadowed room tonight and say what a fool this Griff Jordan must be.

Because they needed supplies at Chainlink, Griff went back uptown. He dismounted at the east end of Houston Street when he saw Lisa Benbow coming along the walk. He felt a flush of excitement. She was wearing a dress of green silk, and carrying a bonnet by its velvet ties. The dress looked new. And as she approached he was aware of a sharp primitive jealousy of the man who would one day take her to wife, who would know her comforting arms, lying in the darkness of a quiet house, making their plans for a future. A man who would build a life with her apart from everyone and everything.

She was humming as she approached and now that she saw him, the song was snatched from her lips. Smiling, he removed his hat. "I hope I didn't destroy your good mood."

She averted her gaze. "Not at all," she said, crisply, and started to move around him on the walk.

Puzzled by her behavior, he frowned. That day when he rode over and had his talk with her, he had the feeling that she found his company not unpleasant. But now—

"May I walk with you?" he asked, and swung in beside her. She was tall, but even so he could look down on the pale sheen of her hair. She halted.

"I think it best that we're not seen together, Mr. Jordan. My brother considers you an enemy. To help keep the peace, let's go our separate ways."

He put on his hat. "I knew your brother is my enemy. I hoped we could be friends."

She went on down the walk while he stood rigid, red-faced from her rebuff. At the gate in a picket fence surrounding a two-story house, she paused and looked back, then hurried into the house.

Griff turned to angle over to the West Texas Store and ran into Sheriff Sam Enright. The sheriff passed the time of day, then mentioned that Lisa Benbow was sure a good-looking girl, but Clyde kept such a tight rein on her that likely she'd never have a chance to get married.

Enright pointed the stub of a cold cigar at the house where Lisa had disappeared. "Clyde bought it for her. Claimed she was too good to live out at the 'Little Place.' I hear that dress is new. Silk. Cost eighteen dollars."

"Benbow takes care of his sister. That's the only decent thing about him."

"Damn generous packing house that Clyde's got his rope tied to. First time I ever heard of loanin' a man money for a beef herd he don't own, to graze on land that was sold out from under him."

"A lot of Yanks think they can get rich on

Texas cattle," Griff said, watching the sheriff's narrow face.

Enright pitched his cigar into the street where it was crushed by the hoofs of a freight team pulling a big-wheeled wagon. "By the way," the sheriff said, "how did the major pay for Chain-link? Cash or check?"

"Cash."

The sheriff pursed his lips. "I know Leithbut never had any use for banks." Enright's gaze lifted to Griff's face. "They say he went to Frisco. If he's headin' that way he's sure stayin' clear of every town. I hear he didn't even go through Paso on his way north. I been asking a few questions here and there. Wrote some letters."

"Leithbut a special friend of yours?"

"He was a money-suckin' leech. But nobody's seen hide nor hair of him or the Oakum boys he took along."

"At the last minute Leithbut changed his mind about Frisco," Griff said. "He headed for Mexico."

"Ah. Maybe that explains him disappearing. Maybe it don't."

Griff met the sheriff's suspicious eyes. "If

108

you've got something on your mind, let's hear it."

Enright spat in the direction of his crushed cigar in the street. "Wouldn't be the first time a man paid over money for somethin' like a ranch the size of Chainlink. Then collected it back in the dark of the moon."

"Take off that badge and tell me that," Griff said angrily.

The sheriff held up a hand in mild protest. "You're too big a man for me to fist fight." He gave Griff a slanted grin. "And I don't figure to try and out-shoot you. Not after you killin' Keller. You got yourself quite a gun rep hereabouts."

"I'm not interested in acquiring that sort of a rep," Griff said stiffly.

"Well, it's that rep, likely, that made Lisa Benbow walk off and leave you standin' foolish awhile ago. There's been a lot of talk around town. Reckon she's heard it. That girl hasn't got much use for gunhands since her brother Tom got killed."

"Can't say I blame her."

"How'd you pay Leithbut? In gold?"

The sheriff had switched the conversation so suddenly that Griff was momentarily at a loss.

His consciousness had been filled with Lisa Benbow. He told Enright that Leithbut had insisted on newly-minted gold. Eighty thousand dollars worth. A wagon had been purchased in Tucson and a false bottom built into it.

"Leithbut loves money more than most men love their wives and kids. But he was also a damn fool. Carryin' that much cash money with only the Oakum brothers—"

Clyde Benbow, coming along the street on a dun and sitting a fancy silver-mounted saddle, caused the sheriff to break off. Benbow reined the horse in at the walk and gave Griff a curt nod.

"See you down at the Del Carmen House," Benbow said to Enright. "Got some things to talk over."

"Sure, Clyde," Enright said easily. "Ain't that a new hoss and saddle?"

"Yeah."

"Sure wish I could get me a fancy beef contract," Enright said, lifted a hand to Griff and then went on down the street, Benbow dismounted now, walking with the sheriff.

In the West Texas Store Griff gave his list to a long-nosed clerk wearing a visor. The clerk seemed overly solicitous. "I hear you out-shot

Keller," the clerk said. "Never liked him much. Always surprised Benbow would keep a man like Keller around on account of Miss Benbow. She's a gentle girl. You just go on about your business and I'll have a wagon sent out with the stuff. You pay in thirty days or we'll carry you longer."

Griff moved to the door and the clerk trailed along, as if experiencing a vicarious thrill in being so close to a man of Griff Jordan's sudden reputation. "You better watch out for Macready and Lawler," the clerk said. "They was good friends of Keller's."

"I've got a hunch they already tried for me once. Since that night I've been wearing one eye in the back of my head."

An exclamation of surprise burst from the clerk. "What's George Wheat lookin' over here for?"

Griff had been in the act of lifting a cracker from the barrel by the door. Now he dropped it and peered through the front window. The towering Wheat was on the opposite walk, looking at the store.

Griff saw the anger on Wheat's broad face, saw the way the large shoulders were tensed, the heavy body hunched forward. Both of

Wheat's big hands were buried in the pockets of a canvas jacket.

"Benbow never should've hired Wheat back," the clerk said, a trace of worry in his voice. "Benbow beat him bloody once. But now him and Wheat are thicker'n flies in the molasses barrel."

When Griff drew his gun and checked the loads, the clerk's eyes showed real fear. "My God, do you and George Wheat figure to tangle?"

"That's up to him," Griff said shortly, and jerking low the brim of his hat to cut the sun, he stepped out of the store.

8

WHEAT glared from the opposite walk. Tension crackled along the street. A man, wearing a leather apron, stepped leisurely out of a saddle shop two doors down on Wheat's side of the street. He stiffened when he saw the two men poised, their eyes raking each other.

And from behind Griff came the store clerk's frantic cry to the man who stood rigid in front of the saddle shop. "Watch it, Leo! There's goin' to be trouble!"

The man in the leather apron sprang to life at the clerk's warning and ducked back into the shop. The shout brought heads popping from doorways. A hotel window banged up. Two men stepped from the cantina down the street. More men came from the Del Carmen House and gathered in a tight knot to peer up the street. Griff could hear the buzz of excited voices.

He crossed to the center of the street and came to a halt, hands loose at his sides. To

Wheat, he said, "I don't know what you've got in mind, but remember this. I let you get your hands on me once. I was lucky that time not to get a broken neck and I know it. I fired you once and it still sticks. And now you're drawing Benbow's pay again. If he's sent you after me, he's wasted his time."

"You think so?"

"I won't fight you. But I'll put a bullet in each knee-cap. That'll slow you up, Wheat. A man shot like that isn't likely to walk again even with crutches. So think it over. I'm not going to fool with you!"

Griff started to turn away, but Wheat stepped from the walk, big booted feet settling into the dust. And Griff thought, The damned fool is going to call my bluff.

There was a terrible rage in Wheat's eyes and his voice shook. "She was cryin'. I was at the house helpin' Clyde move furniture around when she come in. She looked funny and Clyde asks her what's the matter. And she says she wishes you'd never come to Texas at all. She wishes she'd never laid eyes on you. And then she busts out cryin'."

Griff had listened to this, his mouth slowly

114

opening. "You say Lisa wept? She mentioned my name and wept?"

With both hands still buried in the pockets of his canvas jacket, Wheat took a step forward. Not five feet separated them now. A flurry of excitement flashed the length of the street. Down near the stable some riders just coming into town reined in and stood up in their stirrups to see what was going on.

A drop of sweat rolled along one side of Wheat's flattened nose and dropped wetly into a corner of the ugly pattern of his mouth.

While the fact that Lisa had shed tears over him was heartening, he knew there were any number of reasons why she might have wept. Fear for her brother's life now that Griff Jordan had moved to the rangeland . . .

Just because I happened to be lucky and down Keller, he thought, *everybody thinks I'm slicker than bear grease with a gun.*

When Wheat moved forward another step, Griff said, "I've changed my mind. You make one move toward me and I won't shoot for kneecaps now. I'll kill you."

Deliberately Griff turned his back and walked away, moving past the groups of apprehensive spectators.

And as he passed those standing tensely along the street, Griff saw disappointment on some faces. There was little enough happening in a country like this to break the monotony. A fight such as the one that appeared to be shaping up a moment ago would have been feed for the gossips in future months. When a new drummer came to town they'd say, "Hear about the fight we had here?" And the stage passengers would want to hear about it. And maybe even somebody from the El Paso *Advocate* would write about it. And some of those in the crowd had even mentally picked out the spot where Griff Jordan would have been buried. *"We planted him here, stranger. Put up a good fight. But he wasn't no match for George Wheat. That's Wheat over yonder. All scarred to hell and walkin' with a limp. It was a fight, mister. You never seen two grizzly bears go at it any harder than them two."*

And now there was nothing to tell. Because a tall brown-faced man with jingling spurs at his bootheels was turning his back on a taller man who stood uncertainly in the center of the street.

All Griff could think about was to get out of town. There was nothing here for him at the present time. Wheat was unpredictable and if he did ignore Griff's warning and died with Jordan lead in his gut, then there might be some answering to do. And Griff knew there was no telling how a Texas jury might react. Especially if they learned the truth about him. That could make a lot of difference. Men had had their necks broken by the stiffened lever-like wrappings on a hangman's knot on much less provocation. George Wheat's death would be no signal for mourning.

But if there happened to be a trial—just happened to be—then somebody in this vast land embittered from a war that had been lost might look deep into his memory for the name of Jordan. And come up with what they would significantly call the ugly truth. In that event George Wheat would probably be classed as a martyr and the man who killed him ignominiously hanged for the deed.

He was riding across a lot littered with empty whisky bottles and tin cans when he heard a woman call his name. Turning in the saddle, he saw Lisa Benbow in the backyard of the big house he had seen her enter earlier.

Feeling a lift of spirits he reined over and

dismounted by the picket fence that completely surrounded the property.

"I just wanted to warn you about George Wheat," she said in that deep and pleasant voice that thrilled him each time he heard it. "You must understand that he has a very deep feeling towards me—"

"I can understand that," Griff said.

She flashed him a look from under thick lashes. "I was rude to you today. And I'm sorry. In front of George I must have said something, or acted in some way to indicate that you had perhaps insulted me."

He studied her blue eyes, wondering if Wheat could have imagined that Lisa wept. "You possibly shed a few tears?" he said.

She blushed in confusion. "How did you know?"

"Wheat told me."

She looked frightened. "Then you've seen him."

He told her how Wheat had tried to badger him into a fight. "I said I'd kill him if he came for me. I meant it."

"Then you are a gunman," she said. "Just like everyone claims."

"No—"

She stepped back, the flush gone from her face now, her eyes watching him. "I thought when you killed Keller that you were trying to save your life—"

"Wait," he interrupted. "I don't intend to face up to George Wheat. I threatened him and he backed down. Sometimes a man has to use the threat of force. I hope Wheat will keep out of my way. You must realize this, Miss Benbow. I'm just as sick of trouble as you are."

He turned for his horse and twisted the stirrup around for his foot, and she said, "I believe you mean that."

He dropped the stirrup. "I never meant anything more." He came toward her. "Miss Benbow, I—"

She gave a small laugh. "You could call me Lisa. We're practically neighbors, you know."

"Lisa," he said, and there was such intensity in his voice that it seemed to reach her and mold her face suddenly into a pattern that told him he was the man she had been waiting for . . .

"I fought for years against coming back to Texas," he said hoarsely. "Whatever is past or whatever the future holds, it was worth it to look at you now."

"I'll speak to Clyde about firing George Wheat," she said, and turned sideways and pretended to study the picket fence. But he could see the color at her ear lobes and see the pulse at throat and temple. "Wheat means nothing but trouble. And—"

His hands touched her shoulders. He turned her so that they faced each other. She tilted back her head and her lips parted. And in that moment when he bent toward her, she said, her lips barely stirring, "Don't kill my brother. Don't kill Clyde."

He felt a stiffness in his spine, and he halted his forward motion and he saw that her eyes were studying him. He felt a surge of anger.

"Your brother Clyde, sending you—Or was this your own idea? To make a fool of me—"

Still holding her, his head came forward. His face found hers, found the mouth. And the muscles that had held the lips stiff as rope under his own for an instant now went slack. But even as he felt the moment of conquest singing through his blood, she reacted with sudden violence. He felt the knife-like thrust of her small sharp teeth through his lower lip. With a small cry of rage she twisted out of his arms.

"I'm the one who's been made a fool of, Griff Jordan!" she cried. Then he saw the rage die in her eyes to be replaced by sheer terror. "Griff!" she screamed.

He whirled and saw coming toward him at a clumsy run, the towering George Wheat with both hands buried in the pockets of his canvas jacket.

Already Griff was reaching for his gun. But he knew he was too late. Too damned late for living. You could be almighty fast with a gun. You could have the speed of lightning in your hand, but good as you were you couldn't match a man who already had his fingers curled on a trigger.

9

AS it had that day with Keller, instinct saved Jordan. He fell away just enough so that when the right hand pocket of George Wheat's jacket erupted with smoke and flame he heard the ugly *zishhhhhh* of the derringer ball fan the right cheekbone instead of crush it.

Wheat, leaping back now, was struggling to throw off his burning canvas jacket. The whole side of it was smouldering from the powder exploding through the fabric.

A feeling of triumph shot through Griff. He had taken George Wheat's sneak attack and lived. Now he reached for his gun, intending to hold Wheat until the sheriff could be summoned. He intended that Wheat be held for attempted murder.

But the triumph died coldly in him as Lisa cried, "Macready—Lawler! Get away—"

Griff spun but too late. Two men crashed into him from behind with such suddenness that the gun was jarred from his hand and went skating across the ground. He lashed out wildly, heard the sandy-haired Macready's yelp of pain. Then Griff was righting himself.

Dazed, he watched the black-haired Lawler scooping up his fallen gun. And Macready, his nose bloodied from Griff's elbow, had caught Lisa by the wrists and was holding her against the picket fence.

A crowd, attracted by the shot and Lisa's scream, came pounding up from the business district. But Griff had only an instant to see the wide-eyed excited faces bearing down on the clearing behind the Benbow house.

Wheat had drawn the razor from the pocket of the jacket he had discarded. Now with the yellow-boned handle gripped in his right hand, the blade open catching the sunlight, he charged in.

"Oh, my God," Lisa said in a low, horrified voice. "Somebody do something!"

Wheat was yelling at Griff, "You puttin' your hand on her done it! I'd have beat you till you was nothin' but a sack of bones. But now I'm goin' to cut you! Cut you all over!"

As Griff gave ground some of the crowd yelled for Wheat to put up the razor. But Wheat came on, his lips parted, showing teeth as yellowed as the handle of the razor he gripped.

Watching his eyes, Griff backed up. To his right he saw a paling obviously left over when the picket fence was built. He saw Wheat's eyes tighten and then Wheat lunged forward, the razor whipping the air. Griff danced away, snatched up the paling and brought it down hard on Wheat's wrist. The razor fell from his paralyzed fingers.

With a bellow of pain, Wheat spun and ran to grab the razor out of the dust. But an onlooker braved the big man's wrath and beat him to it.

"Knock him loose from his boots, Jordan!" the man yelled.

Griff, closing fast, struck Wheat on the side of the head. It was a tremendous smash but Wheat only staggered a little, then whirled and tried to grab Griff by the neck. Griff dodged away from him.

Lisa cried, "Clyde will fire you for this!" She was trying to free herself from Macready.

Lawler was grinning with his scarred mouth as the two combatants circled. "Clyde will pay a bonus for this, you mean," he told her.

Slowly Wheat circled Griff, who stood stiffly.

The crowd grew and the murmur of excited voices droned in the hot still air.

Suddenly Wheat lunged in, arms flailing. Griff ducked a right, pivoting as Wheat plunged past, drove in a solid smash to the inverted V below the rib box. Before Wheat could back off, Griff hit him again. The crowd was yelling. Wheat, his thick forearms crossed over his belly, gave ground as Griff pounded him.

"You got him on the run, Jordan!" a man shouted.

As Wheat tried to kick him in the groin, Griff dodged and brought up his own foot. But Wheat had been waiting for him: he caught the foot in his two hands and twisted it cruelly. Griff, hopping on one foot, felt as if a white hot sliver of iron had been driven into the leg Wheat was twisting.

With a bellow of triumph Wheat began to spin and Griff's other foot left the ground. He was whirling slowly at first, then faster, as a boy might swing a weighted rope around and around. Blood rushed to his head and he found his arms flung out wide from his body, helpless.

Griff Jordan was being spun like a toy. Wheat was yelling insanely, head thrown back, the sound bubbling up from his chest like the roar of a wounded bear.

As he came whirling around, Griff's outstretched fingers brushed the pickets of the fence. The next time around he caught at a paling that came free in his hands. The sudden jar threw Wheat off balance. Griff kicked free and got up but he was so dizzy from the spin that the earth tilted and he found himself with the sun in his eyes.

"Roll away from him!" somebody cried, and Lisa's scream of warning knifed into his consciousness. He saw Wheat looming up like a huge black cloud between himself and the sun. Feet off the ground, coming down swiftly, all that bulk aimed for Griff's chest.

Twisting aside, Griff evaded the full impact, but one of the heels tore skin from his right side as if it had been peeled with a knife.

But the pain helped anchor his senses. Shakily he got to his feet. Wheat knocked him down. He struggled to his knees. Wheat came in with lifted knee. Jerking his head aside, Griff caught Wheat by the leg and yanked hard. As Wheat fell face down Griff was on him, bending an arm up behind the broad back.

"Give me a gun, somebody," Griff panted. "I've had enough of this."

But if anyone intended to stop what was certain in the minds of the assemblage to be a massacre, Wheat settled it. With a sudden whiplike movement of his big body he twisted over on his back and Griff was forced to let go of the arm. He fell some distance away.

They both got slowly to their feet at the same time. Griff could feel blood soaking into his shirt from the wound in his side where Wheat's bootheel had torn the skin. He braced himself for another charge and managed to nail Wheat with a solid right. Wheat went back on his heels and fought for balance.

As Griff moved in he was aware of a thunderous roar in his ears. He saw beyond the bleeding mask of Wheat's face that he struck repeatedly, the flushed excited faces of the onlookers.

One of Griff's blows moved Wheat's nose off center. Another split the lips across the blunt and yellowed teeth. But as Griff came in Wheat suddenly brought down his head, the crown smashing Griff on the forehead. He felt as if he had been hit with a stone hammer. He felt his legs collapsing. There was nothing to see but blackness. Terror gripped him.

He could feel dirt under his fingers. Hard Texas ground under his chest and knees. He was down.

Blindly he looked around and the first glimpse of the earth moved into the terrible blackness that had curtained his eyes. And the first glimpse could very well be his last. For he knew he was kneeling on the ground now. And the first thing he saw was a thick knee lifting toward his face. It crashed into him and he went over backwards. Wheat plunged down on him.

In one screaming gust of pain and nausea his breath was jarred out of him. As they struggled on the ground, he instinctively groped with his fingers across Wheat's bloodied face. He found the softness of eyes. But before he could press in, his wrist was caught and twisted. In that moment he drove his knee upward and heard Wheat's sharp cry of pain. Wheat rolled away and thrashed upon the ground.

Griff got up, his knees wobbly and threatening to give out.

"Kick him bloody!" a man yelled. "It's what he'd do to you!"

Fighting off the weakness, Griff staggered

forward. Wheat lay face down on the ground. Griff knew there was no longer any question of fighting fair. Of giving Wheat any advantage whatsoever. It was end it now or die.

But Wheat suddenly sprang to life and came in swiftly, clawing for Griff's throat. Their fingers shredded the clothing that covered their upper bodies. Their torsos glistened with sweat.

Blindly Griff struck out and felt his knuckles smack with a wet solidness against jawbone. Just as he thought he had hurt Wheat, the big man hit him under the heart. Desperately Griff clung on. He felt his legs going again. Over Wheat's shoulder he saw Lisa's frightened eyes. Maybe it was seeing her, or hearing the sound of the crowd gone mad that helped him fight over the encroaching darkness. He spun away from Wheat's grasp. Then he turned quickly to meet Wheat's charge.

He lashed out at the swollen face of the big man. The force of the blow, coupled with Wheat's momentum, turned it into a deadly thing. Wheat's body shuddered, the eyes opened wide. As Wheat came to a halt and tried to measure Griff, he was hit again. And again. Griff flailed away until somebody grabbed him.

Only then did he realize he was lashing out at the air. Wheat lay on the ground, unconscious.

He didn't remember much more until he found himself lying on a wooden table in a room that smelled of disinfectant. Doc Purcell, bald head gleaming in a shaft of sunlight, was probing for broken ribs and then binding up the gash in Griff's side.

"You and your partner," Purcell said with a shake of his head. "You both get yourselves beaten half to death. Don't you know enough to wear a gun?"

"I'll carry a spare after this, Doc. I won't go through the meat chopper again. Not for George Wheat or anybody else."

"You're the first man to tangle with Wheat that I've ever been able to patch up."

Although the doctor advised Griff to stay there for the night, he would have none of it. Stiff and sore, his right eye swollen almost shut, the backs of his hands raw from pounding Wheat's face, Griff staggered out. There was still a crowd around the doctor's house and when they saw Griff they came up, whooping like small boys.

Griff knew right then that if Del Carmen were the state of Texas and he were running for governor he'd be elected unanimously. One of them had brought up his horse and he climbed into the saddle, wondering if he could hang on long enough to reach Chainlink.

Then he saw Sheriff Sam Enright coming up. "I told Wheat to get out of town and stay out," the sheriff said.

"You could have told him that *before* the fight."

"I didn't know you and him had at it till I got back. I went out with Benbow to his place. He wanted to show me that bull he bought from old man Goodrich."

"Convenient time to be out of town."

"Now don't get me tied into this, Jordan. Everybody knows I don't play Benbow's game."

"Everybody knows his old man put you in office."

Griff never got to Chainlink that day. Miguel Aleman, the only hand old man Goodrich had left on his place, found him leading a lame horse and gave him a lift in his wagon to the ranch on Median Creek.

Clyde Benbow took one look at George Wheat, lying unconscious on a pile of hay at the rear of the stable, and began to swear. Macready and Lawler were there giving him the details of the historic battle.

"I figured when I came back to town, Griff Jordan would have his brains kicked out," Clyde Benbow said darkly.

"Jordan's too damned lucky to live," Macready said.

Benbow looked at the sandy-haired gunman. "I saw Jordan heading out of town. How about you and Lawler making sure he doesn't get where he's going?"

Lawler spat from a corner of his scarred mouth. "He ain't nobody to fool with, Clyde."

"Just because you missed him in the lamplight that night is no sign you can't finish him," Benbow said.

"Then why don't you do it?"

"I want to keep clear on account of my sister." He glared down at the beaten hulk of George Wheat. "That's why I got out of town when Jordan and Wheat tangled."

"You knew they was goin' at it?"

"I got Wheat stirred up a little over Lisa." Benbow added, "I'll take George down to the shack along the river and keep him hid out. Enright told him not to come back to town. By the time I get back I want Jordan in a pine box."

"You been buyin' a house, a bull, some cows and a new saddle, Clyde," Macready said. "How about buyin' us for the job?"

Benbow's gray eyes studied him a moment. "Five hundred dollars worth of buying suit you?"

"Yeah," Lawler said, and gave Macready a tight grin, "providin' we get it ahead of time. If I'm goin' to risk my neck I want my belly warmed with good whisky. And right at this minute I'm broke as the day before payday."

Benbow dug a hand in his pocket and passed out some newly-minted gold coins.

10

THE Goodrich ranch had gone to seed. The back part of the sod-roofed house had been closed off so there wouldn't be much to clean. Goodrich's vaquero, Miguel, slept in the bunkhouse that once had held twenty men. The barn roof was half-gone, blown off in a storm of two years ago. Only eight horses were in the corral that formerly held a hundred.

In the kitchen Goodrich cooked up a pot of coffee and when it was done, laced it with whisky. All the while Griff had talked, telling of his troubles since coming to this desolate stretch of country known as the Bend, of his fight with Wheat. Goodrich seemed unable to believe that a human being had finally been able to whip the big man.

"I figured the only thing that'd set him down," the gray-haired rancher said, "was a grizzly bear backed up by a mountain lion or two."

"I can't believe it myself," Griff said and felt of his aching jaws.

"If Wheat looks worse'n you do, he must be a rare sight."

Griff drank off one cup of the spiked coffee and felt life begin to struggle through his bruised body again. On the second cup he abruptly asked Goodrich about the team of black horses the major had purchased from him.

"I hear folks think Major Clay paid too much for that team," Goodrich said, and gave Griff a slanted look across the spur-scarred kitchen table.

"So they say."

Old man Goodrich, who had spent a good chunk of his life squinting against the glare of the Texas sun, now seemed intent on digging Texas soil from under his broken nails with the point of a *cuchillo*.

"Guess I did cut a long stick with them black hosses. But they're a prime pair. Bought 'em for my wife, Jordan. I always promised her a team like that. It was one of the things I promised when we was married. A long time ago, Jordan. I was a little late. That's the trouble with a lot of us. Always a little late."

"Yeah," Griff agreed, and thought of his own life.

"That's the trouble with this country," Goodrich said sadly. "A man's so busy stayin' alive he forgets the things that bring pleasure to a woman." He blew his nose on an old bandanna.

They had more whisky and coffee and then Goodrich, who had been studying Griff closely, said, "Knew some Jordans once. Down in the brush country. Any kin of yours."

Griff sipped the scalding concoction of oily coffee and cheap whisky. "Could be. Jordan's a name that's common enough."

Goodrich leaned across the table. "The old man made a fortune in hides before the war. Bullhide Jordan, they called him. Had two sons. The Jordans come from Boston, so I hear."

"That so?"

"The old man had two sons. One brother went with Hood. Hear he got killed when Sherman hit Atlanta."

Griff finished his cup of coffee and whisky.

Goodrich said, "The other brother went north. Fought against his own people."

Griff sank back in his chair. In the yard

Miguel was singing a Mexican song to the accompaniment of a guitar with a broken string.

"Maybe this younger brother you speak of," Griff said tensely, "remembered the Yankee grandfather who brought the black men to this country in chains. Maybe he felt ashamed of this grandfather. Like Bullhide Jordan felt ashamed of his father and came to Texas to get away from him. And maybe when the war broke out this younger son of Bullhide Jordan went north. To fight for some of those black men Grandfather Jordan had a hand in chaining." He sat stiffly, right hand near his gun butt.

Goodrich shrugged his bony shoulders. "I'm North myself, lad. Was once, anyhow. I come south to fight with Taylor in the Mexican War. Deserted. I ain't proud of it. But I couldn't stomach the way we treated the Mexicans. I married one of 'em. My wife was a Velasquez." He took a long drink, then set the tin cup back on the table. "The good Lord punished me for desertin', maybe. We never had no kids, me and Maria. That's punishment enough for any man." Then he added, "No kids of our own, that is."

Griff sensed an opening to discuss Maydelle,

but he held off. "I wonder how many others around here will connect me up with the Texas Jordans?"

"You better hope nobody else." The gray head shook slowly back and forth. "But I reckon it's only the real old-timers that'd remember your pa, Bullhide. Why didn't you change your name?"

"A man might as well turn his back on his family as to change his name."

"I hear old Bullhide cashed in 'bout ten years back." When Griff nodded, the rancher said, "How come you rode back here to Texas, anyhow?"

"I was never happy anywhere else. I saw a chance to come back and—"

"Tied in with that Major Clay, huh? Never laid eyes on him, but I hear he made a million dollars in silver."

"He made a lot, that's for sure."

"Don't blame you for stringin' with a gent like that. A man can cut a lot of distance off the trail of his life if he can weight his pockets with a little gold."

They had been drinking steadily and Griff felt some of the ache go out of his body under the influence of the whisky. Then, as darkness

138

approached Goodrich cooked up a supper of frijoles, carne seca and chilis. He went to the door and yelled for Miguel to come in and eat with them. The vaquero didn't answer. Closing the door Goodrich muttered something about Miguel having a sweetheart down along the river.

When supper was over Griff and the old man sat in the dark, watching through the kitchen window the west rim of the horizon turn gold, then silver. And the world moved up into darkness and the stars came out with their silvered Texas intensity.

Griff said, "Ever hear of a man named Sam Kinsfather?"

"Why for you ask about him?" Goodrich's voice was hard with suspicion.

"Heard talk about him in town."

"Been a long time since I heard that name. Most twenty years. Didn't know anybody remembered him. A cold-hearted killer, was Sam Kinsfather."

"I hear he was tied in some way with Maydelle Ashley."

Goodrich leaped to his feet, his chair flung back. "So that's why you come? To draw me out about Maydelle?"

"I feel sorry for her."

"You've seen her?" Goodrich cried.

"I've talked with her."

"You know what I mean when I say have you *seen* her!"

"I've talked to her. Nothing more. Just talk."

With a gusty sigh Goodrich picked up his chair and sat down. The silence thickened as did the shadows. Horses stirred in the corral outside.

"You got to forgive an old man," Goodrich said. "In my day there was only two kinds of women. The good kind you knew was straight. You knew it like you know your own name. And the other kind, well, they was born to it. But now'days things is different. I don't know what the world is comin' to. I truly don't. How a good, sweet girl like Maydelle—"

There was a tense silence in the dark of the kitchen. Under the stove lids a faint glow of a dying cook fire threw dancing shadows on the walls.

"I talk tough," Goodrich said, "but I got mush in the gut. If I didn't I'd take a gun and kill that bastard Clyde Benbow!"

"He the one that—made her this way?"

"She had his kid when she was sixteen. The

140

kid died. I—" He stood, a hunched old man, all the strength and bitterness suddenly drained out of him. "If only he'd married her. I tried to send her away, for Maria's sake. But Maydelle come back. She wanted to be near Clyde."

"She still love him?" Griff asked in surprise.

"God knows why, but I'm afraid she does."

Griff shook his head. "Some women like to have a fist in their face. Why, I don't know."

"Maria and I counted on Maydelle gettin' married. We raised her like our own. She come to us when her ma died, Jordan. This Sam Kinsfather you was talkin' about was her uncle. Her mother's brother. He follered his sister and her husband here and killed the husband in a fight. And it wasn't long till the mother died. And that little tyke had nobody. Her uncle never come back. So me and Maria took her in. We wasn't young then, neither. But we took a tuck in our lives and brought up the girl. And we lived for the day when she'd get married and bring her own kids home for a visit." Goodrich lit a lamp and absently brushed crumbs from the table into his hand. Then he threw the crumbs on the floor. "It was Maydelle turnin' out like this that kilt Maria. My wife just give

141

up. It was a long sickness with the woman. Clyde Benbow kilt my Maria, just as sure as if he'd hit her with an ax."

"Yet you sell him a bull. And I hear talk you're going to lease him land."

Goodrich sank to his chair, his lips split in an ugly smile. "If he keeps on he'll hang himself. That's all I'm livin' for. To see him hang."

In the morning after breakfast Griff managed to saddle a borrowed horse. His fingers were still stiff from the fight with Wheat. But a good night's sleep had refreshed him.

Goodrich said, "I done some thinkin' last night. I figure to ride over one of these days and have a look at your Major Clay."

Griff climbed stiffly into the saddle. His side pained. "I gave Maydelle Ashley a thousand dollars. I hope she'll get out of town for a spell."

"Was it your money or the major's?" Goodrich demanded.

"Mine," Griff said, and saw the old man's face lose some of its tension. "I'm the major's partner, Goodrich. I aim to stay here a long time. I'm back home in Texas and for the first time in years I've got the sun in my face.

Nobody is going to ruin things for me. Nobody."

"If you done what you say you did for Maydelle, then I admire you. I'll keep my mouth shut about you bein' old Bullhide Jordan's boy. But one of these days I'll ride over and have a talk with your friend Sam Kinsfather."

"A man must feel shame, deep shame, to change his name." Griff reined the horse away from the old man. "The major wants to right any wrongs he committed in the past. For one thing he overpaid you for your horses. So let him do things in his own way."

The old man's gaze hardened. "You think his money will take the bed off that girl's back?"

"Maybe it's a little late to right all the wrongs. But everything the major has done here in Texas is for that girl."

Griff lifted a hand and spurred out of the yard. Despite the beating he had suffered, his spirits were lighter. Before he had been in the dark. But now he had a basis for discussion with Major Milo Clay. Before this day was out the major, drunk or sober, would bring Maydelle Ashley out to Chainlink.

11

THE spot picked for the ambush by the two men was as nearly perfect as those things can be. It was at the foot of a canyon trail where mesquites grew thick, throwing gnarled shadows on the ground. On the slopes huisache was green in the sunlight that now was creeping slowly down the western wall of the canyon. With their horses nose-wrapped and downwind from the approaching rider, Macready and Lawler cradled their rifles behind a row of boulders and waited. From the vantage point where they had observed the Goodrich ranch all night, they had seen Griff leave and head this way to pick up the Chain-link trail.

Macready laughed quietly. "Wait'll Clyde hears how we sneaked up and got an earful of the palaver last night."

"I don't worry a damn about this now," Art Lawler said, his scarred mouth smiling. "Nobody's goin' to give much of a damn what happens to a rotten turncoat like the son of Bullhide Jordan."

"A man keeps his ear close to the wall long enough," Macready said softly, "an' he sure learns a lot. I never figured Clyde was the first with Maydelle."

"Had Clyde's kid, by God."

"Next time I go down there I'll call her Maw."

Lawler had removed his hat and placed it on the ground by the large rock that shielded them from the descending trail. "She don't look like she ever borned a kid. There ain't no sag to her anywhere at all."

"Maybe we better not let on to Clyde we heard old Goodrich talkin' about Maydelle. You never know about Clyde."

"Yeah. He might bust a hole in a man before he can finish takin' his second breath."

They heard a faint sound in the distance and Lawler whispered tensely, "Remember, we do this easy, see? We wait till he's twenty yards away and then cut loose."

"I hope he don't die right off. I want him to know we're doin' it for Keller."

"We're doin' it for five hundred dollars,"

Lawler said, giving the sandy-haired Macready a faint grin.

"Yeah. Keller wasn't a man to shed no tears over, at that."

"You remember how Keller died," Lawler reminded quietly. "How Keller had his gun already out when Jordan shot him. Then maybe you won't let that redhaired temper of yours set you off too soon and give away the game."

Macready grunted that he wasn't such a damned fool that he'd go off half-cocked and endanger their lives.

"This Jordan is boot leather tough," Lawler said. "We want to be damn sure of him."

They waited tensely, certain that Griff Jordan would not fail to come this way, for it was the shortest route to Chainlink headquarters. They had trailed him yesterday to the Goodrich ranch and waited outside all night. Their orders from Benbow were to bury Jordan where he fell and take his horse and saddle and themselves to Mexico. And lose the horse and saddle down there. In a few months they could come back, for by that time Benbow would again have possession of Chainlink. Nobody would ever know what happened to Griff Jordan, who had gone north to fight against his own people.

"You're sweatin', Art," Macready whispered with a tight grin.

"So are you."

Watching the house all night had thinned their nerves and given them the jumps. They'd not even had the solace of drink, and no breakfast to ease their grumbling stomachs.

Lawler marked the spot in the trail twenty yards away with his eyes. A sotol bush grew there and presently, if all went well, a dying man would thrash down on it.

It couldn't miss. It just couldn't. Yet Lawler was remembering the moment at Elvine's Store when Keller spun with a revolver in hand to cut down the tall stranger. And instead had himself been cut down.

A drop of sweat fell from Lawler's forehead onto the barrel of his rifle. Lawler wiped it off, polished the barrel with his palm.

In that moment he again heard the sound that had drifted to them before, nearer now. The sound of a hoof clacking on rock. He wished now he had suggested they take up positions that would command Griff Jordan's back instead of his front. Even with two rifles in experienced hands, it was more comforting to have a man like Griff Jordan going away from you than coming toward you. A man like that had too much luck. First Keller, and then surviving a hand-to-hand encounter with George Wheat. It seemed incredible for one man to have such fantastic good fortune. But such things must end. And there was no doubt that Jordan's hands would be stiff and swollen from the fight with Wheat. That slowed a man down if he tried to reach for a gun. But Jordan would have no chance to reach for anything.

"Here he comes," Lawler said uneasily. "Now remember what I said. Don't do some damn fool thing. Wait till he's by that sotol bush. Twenty yards away."

"I could kill him at a hundred." Macready's voice was shaking.

"I said twenty." Another drop of sweat fell to the rifle barrel which Lawler quickly smeared with the palm of his hand.

Griff Jordan appeared in a shaft of morning sunlight and came down the trail into the sudden shadows along the west wall.

A bead of briny sweat dropping from a man's brow to the sun-warmed barrel of a rifle; then the sunlight catching the drop of salted moisture at just the right angle as it touched metal. A brief, dim and distant flash. Then nothing.

To a man of Griff Jordan's background it could mean many things. The sun touching a whisky flask discarded by some previous rider through the canyon. Perhaps light reflected on a tin can. Or—

He reined in on the trail, a good seventy-five yards from the canyon floor and the spot where a sotol bush struggled up through the rocky Texas soil.

And this reining in of the roan, the sudden kneeing it off the trail onto a shelf bordered by mesquite brought an instant reaction from below.

Macready impatiently thrust up his sandy-haired head to see what had caused the big man to turn off the trail. Lawler, who had been smearing the drop of sweat along the rifle barrel, turned suddenly, cursing so loudly Griff could hear him: "Down, you damn fool!" And Lawler's black head with the neatly parted hair, was revealed. Lawler was frantically jerking at Macready's shirt sleeve with his left hand, while swinging the rifle into position with his right.

Macready, off balance from Lawler's jerking on his arm, spoiled the first shot. It went hammering high into the mesquites that bordered the shelf, cutting twigs and dropping them on Griff Jordan's wide shoulders. He was down off the roan and working in the first shell. With a steady pressure on the trigger he sent it screaming downward into and through the puff of gunsmoke. Into and through Macready's face. The man's upper body fell loosely across the rocky barricade, arms dangling. There was a sudden bright splash of blood across the stone.

Lawler was leaping back and to one side, firing his rifle. And because from Lawler's position he had a good clear target of the man no longer screened by mesquite, the shot counted. Griff felt the numbing shock in his right arm, the force of the projectile twisting him to his knees. He dropped the rifle which he had been swinging to cover Lawler. Cursing, he reached for it just as a rattle of hoofbeats came from below. He saw Lawler burst from cover, flat against the neck of a dun horse.

The dun lunged, screamed at the tearing spur rowels on the boots of the frantic man with the scarred mouth. In a thundering rage at the cowardly attempt to murder him from ambush, Griff fired the rifle with his left hand. But no accuracy was possible shooting one-handed at this range. He saw Lawler disappear on the racing dun at a bend in the trail. To emerge later, a half mile away. Then he was gone altogether.

Nauseated with shock, Griff tore out the sleeve of his shirt. He could see the ugly trench where the heavy-caliber slug had torn flesh and bone. But it had gone clear through, if that was any consolation. With his bandanna he managed to fashion a tourniquet. But even with the bleeding checked he felt light in the head. Looking down at the ground at his feet, he was surprised at the blood he had lost. Dry-mouthed, he staggered to his roan and booted the rifle and tried to swing aboard. But the roan was spooked by the scent of blood and it took three tries with "Hold still, you crazy bastard," before he cleared the leather and got his one-armed seat. He rode slowly down the trail. The roan's rump swung off the trail, the rear hoofs trampling into green pulp the sotol that had been intended to mark the spot where he was going to die.

But Griff Jordan knew only that he was ill and lucky to be alive on this bright Texas day. Into the early morning, preoccupied with what he had learned at the Goodrich ranch, he had ridden. And death had come sickeningly close. Just a few inches to the left and the bullet would have mangled a lung instead of an arm.

His belly lurched and he could taste the sour aftermath of fear as he neared Macready, draped like an empty sack over some rocks. The smell of death tightened the roan's muscles and Griff, a small panic burgeoning, forced himself to speak softly, soothingly, "Easy, boy. Easy now—" because if the horse should run he knew he didn't have the strength to keep his balance.

He didn't have the strength to cover Macready's body, nor did he have the urge. They had meant to murder him. But he did find the man's horse tied off in the brush and managed to free it and send it rocketing along the canyon.

Griff rode out, the shock gone now, the pain an avalanche smothering him with its intensity. He drew his revolver and held it and the reins with his left hand. It was possible Lawler might try his murderous game again. If he did, Griff prayed he would try it up close enough for revolver range.

But when he emerged from the canyon and saw the tawny desolation of Texas stretching flat and unlovely all the way to the blue barrier of the Chisos he saw no sign of a rider.

"Lawler!" he cried. "Come out! Show yourself!"

The voice was not his own, but a thin sound that somehow reminded him of the distant shout of a sick old man.

He squinted his eyes against the distortions of landscape. The ground seemed to heave and there was a thickness to the very air.

"Damn, damn," he said under his breath in his thin, fever-tight voice. "Why does a man have to come home to Texas?"

He stared out at the ugly land with the purple haze of distant mountains at the end of the world. Why had he come back here when common sense should have shown him that he faced a house deck with more aces than a man could bet against? Where the story of Bullhide Jordan would still be told by the old-timers like Goodrich. Bullhide Jordan and his two sons, one in a hero's grave as a defender of Atlanta. The other, the one they didn't talk about, the one who put on Billy Boy blue and carried gun and sword against Texas. Coming back to a country where a man could shove a gun into his belly and say, "You treacherous dog," and pull the trigger and likely be given a medal for the deed.

A man like the one named Keller, buried now. Or like the one named Macready, unburied but just as dead. Or the one named Art Lawler, now hugging the neck of a frantic horse.

And behind these men, two dead and one with the raw sickness of fear in his guts, was Clyde Benbow. And in the feverish light of Griff's brain he clearly saw Benbow's sullen handsome face. And he imagined then that he methodically emptied his gun into the face, as a man might fire at a melon lying beside the trail. And behind the shattered unrecognizable face was Lisa Benbow, screaming horribly at all that remained of her brother.

He began to laugh but the jolting of his body put a grinding pain along his nerves and into his teeth.

So he had come back to Texas to face his ancient enemies who would curse him for what they considered treachery. Back to face the new enemies he had made.

And here he was with the only talent he possessed, gone forever now in the shattered arm that hung like a weighted something tied to his body by a rope. As useless a something as it was possible for a man to possess.

12

THE major's first act upon arising that morning was to pour out the rest of the quart of whisky into a wash basin with small roses painted on the sides. Then the major lurched to a window and opened it and threw the bottle into the yard. Yes, Griff, when he got home, would be proud of him.

The major put on his best suit of black broadcloth, the one he had worn during the long night when he had seen his fortunes rise to such dizzy heights on the Virginia City Exchange. It was his lucky suit, and this was to be his lucky day.

He brushed his hair, smoothed his mustache and took a look at himself in a wall mirror. His face was almost healed from the fists of the dead Keller. He wondered how Griff looked this morning. Word had come from town about the historic battle between Griff and George Wheat. They said Griff was able to sit a saddle all right, but at the last moment he had likely thought it wiser to stay in town. George Wheat, so the report went, had gone to hole up somewhere along the river and nurse his wounds.

Griff had taken the burdens so far in this venture, the major thought. It was high time that Major Milo Clay did likewise.

Milo Clay, he thought with a wry grin. A name he had picked off a fence on a wild flight east years ago. *Milo Clay's Remedy*. The grin faded as the other name crossed his mind. Sam Kinsfather. So long since a man had called him that. Twenty years. Then he had come west from Virginia, hunting the scoundrel who had run off with his young sister. A man named Ashley. Tracing them finally to a cluster of mud huts with no name. A town later to be known as Del Carmen. And there finding that his sister had given birth to a daughter. The trail had been long; the girl now was three years old. He had found his sister and the daughter alone in a shack, and the major remembered how he had become sick to his stomach at the ravages which four years' living with Si Ashley had put on her face.

Her face was bruised, for Si Ashley had beaten her that morning. He'd been a buffalo hunter of sorts, recently drifting to West Texas to trade with the Comanches. The major looked for a ring on his sister's finger and found none.

Then Ashley came in and there was a brief struggle. A gun went off and Si Ashley fell dead.

And the sister, instead of being thankful, went into hysterics and threw herself upon the body of the man who had mistreated her for so long. She suddenly snatched up a shotgun and tried to kill her brother. When the major disarmed her, she ran screaming from the house, and a group of Ashley's friends got a rope and chased him for miles. He saved his neck by getting into Mexico.

For years he vowed he would return and do something for this niece he had seen only once. But the war had intervened and a man had no money at all when it was over. And life itself was very nearly over, for in the closing days the fighting was bitter. And when the major's troops were at last overrun there were many irregularities in the matter of taking prisoners.

The casualties had been extremely heavy. When at last the hill they were fighting to take had been captured, the men in blue brought in an uncommon few live prisoners. The major, the officer of highest rank left alive, was about to be stood against a tree and shot. A young lieutenant had fought his way and with saber beaten off his own men and announced, "The major is my prisoner."

After the war they saw each other many times. The fact that Griff Jordan, a native Texan, had fought for the North, did not lower him in the major's eyes. For Major Milo Clay from the first had considered the Rebellion a stupid and utterly wasteful venture.

Following the war he had dedicated himself to making a stake. He made a small one in Frisco and lost it. Drifting to Virginia City, he managed to ride the silver boom to its peak. Then he had written Griff Jordan to join him. And while Griff purchased a herd in Tucson and hired men, the major had come back to Del Carmen to look around.

He had found his niece. And learned why she had become a woman living at the end of Rojo Street. She was a daughter of Velma Kinsfather, of the Virginia Kinsfathers. Maydelle Ashley, born out of wedlock. The same as her own son, sired by Clyde Benbow. Maydelle had nothing left but the Ashley name, which was not legally hers. Her son had not lived.

Each time the major was about to make

himself known to her, his nerve failed. Liquor seemed the only solution.

But this morning and from now on all was to be different. He'd fight in the open. He wouldn't buy his way as he had intended. Buying horses from old man Goodrich, paying too much, because he had learned the old man had raised Maydelle. Buying Chainlink because he knew it was the one thing that would hurt Benbow more than anything else.

He would take a gun and face Benbow. He would say, "Sir, you have ruined my niece," and shoot him.

The major turned after studying his shaking hands. He looked at the wash basin filled with whisky. Well, perhaps one drink to steady his nerves. Only one drink.

Then after he'd taken a gun and settled his score with Benbow, he'd go to the end of Rojo Street and bring Maydelle home. And when Maydelle had become rich overnight, the citizens of Del Carmen would begin to respect her.

Even as the major took his first drink from the crockery basin tilted to his lips, he felt the fear growing. The fear and the shame.

When Ed Damon looked in on him later he was surprised to find the major, fully clothed,

160

lying across the bed, an empty water basin resting on his chest.

On this morning Clyde Benbow made sure that George Wheat was on his way to a shack made of slabs of shale, far down in the willows along the river. He told Wheat to stay out of sight for a time until certain matters were adjusted. Wheat, barely able to hold himself upright in the saddle, mumbled something under his breath and started south.

When Benbow saw his sister that morning he knew from the fury in her eyes what to expect. And he began carefully to build his defenses.

"I hope you're satisfied!" Lisa cried. "Sicking George Wheat on Jordan."

"I didn't have a thing to do with it." Benbow spread his hands, trying to make his voice convincing.

They were in the parlor of the big house he had bought for her. "I ran Wheat out," Benbow went on. "This time for good."

"Very convenient that you talked the sheriff into going out to the ranch and looking at your prize bull. You knew George was going to fight Jordan."

Clyde Benbow gave her a searching look. "How come you care what happens to Jordan?"

"I won't stand for this sort of thing, Clyde!" Her mouth was white. "I'm not going to see the Benbows live as they did in Poppa's time. Not with a gun in one hand and a rope in the other."

"You got not one damn thing to say about it, Lisa!" This talk of Jordan angered him.

"I may go to Austin to live, Clyde," she said abruptly. "I've been thinking about it for quite awhile."

He had been taking an angry hitch at his pants. Now his hands dropped to his sides. "Why you want to go there? You've got this house. I bought it for you."

"Some of the Benbows have run to Austin in the past. When they were in trouble."

His eyes were tight and watchful. "What's that supposed to mean?"

"I'm thinking of a time when Maydelle and I used to ride together a lot. We were just kids. And I remember her coming out to Chainlink one morning, crying. And you had some words with her. And the next thing I knew you were gone. Tom said you went to Austin on business.

162

You didn't come back in months. By that time Maydelle had her baby."

Benbow looked away. "I didn't think you knew."

"Part of it I guessed." She stepped forward and put a hand on his arm. "I'm not condemning you for something that happened years ago. We can't change that. I have no respect for Maydelle for what she's done. And I know why she did it. Hoping to disgrace herself under your very nose. Hoping to get back at you that way. But she doesn't know you like I do. You don't give a damn."

"I don't like you swearing," he said sharply.

"If I go to Austin you can send me enough money to live on. If not, then I'll find a job."

"No Benbow woman ever worked!"

"This one will!" She faced up to him. "Either that, Clyde, or you make your peace with Griff Jordan."

"By God, he's out to wreck us! Can't you see that?"

"I see nothing of the kind. Major Clay bought Chainlink from its legal owner and made Griff Jordan a foreman-partner. And you're not man enough to admit that Chainlink is gone."

"I'm going to have that ranch back, Lisa,"

he said in a quiet, deadly voice. "I never meant anything so much in my life."

She gave a quick shake of her blond head. "We have a chance to be something again, Clyde. But not on Chainlink. Take the money you're getting from Chicago and lease the land from Goodrich like you planned. You've got a good start with that bull. Buy some cows. We can build again. We don't need Chainlink."

Benbow looked away, his face dark with anger. "Chainlink has always been Benbow. It'll never be anything else."

Her voice softened. "Yes, it will, Clyde. It already is something else. You can't change that."

"I'll change it!"

She stepped back. "I won't stand for it, Clyde. Not sending two or three men after one. Like in Poppa's time. Not that!"

"You in love with Jordan or something?"

She almost told him the truth, but something in his eyes frightened her. "I want to live in peace, Clyde. A lot of people hate us Benbows for the things Poppa did."

"And for the things I did." His mouth twisted. "But they don't hate us for the things your precious brother Tom did."

"Why do you always call him my brother? He was as much your brother as he was mine!" She clenched her hands. "Chainlink didn't bring us much happiness. I've reminded you of that. Poppa bet the proceeds from a cattle sale on the turn of a card. And he lost. He shot himself. I saw his body that night, Clyde. I saw Tom's body in the street after that drunken cowboy shot him. I don't want to see you lying dead."

"Or Jordan lying dead."

"Yes, or Jordan," she said. "Make your peace with him."

"And you'll forget this talk about Austin?"

"I'll never leave here."

"You'll always stay with me? You and me together?" He came forward eagerly.

"I'll stay here. But one day I hope to be married. But you'll always be welcome—"

"Welcome!" His eyes were narrowed and ugly. "It is Jordan, isn't it?"

"Talk with him, Clyde. And remember this. No man could ever take your place with me. You're my brother and you'll always have a very special place in my heart."

He snatched his hat from an antler rack in the hall and went out. Lisa watched him through the leaded glass of the front door, a little fearful of what she might have started.

Benbow was playing a desultory stud game with Doc Purcell and a drummer from Paso in the Del Carmen House when one of the Chainlink riders burst in and looked wildly around. Spotting Doc, he came running over through the crowd. "You're wanted at Chainlink. Griff Jordan's had his right arm shot all to rags!"

Purcell, giving Benbow a slanted look, cashed in his chips and followed the rider outside. In a few moments Benbow saw Doc and the rider heading out of town, Doc in his buggy, the Chainlink man in the saddle.

"What you reckon happened to Jordan?" one of the crowd wondered.

With heavy-shouldered arrogance that was a mask for his deep concern, he went to the bar and had a drink. Where were Lawler and Macready? Why the hell was Jordan still alive? He felt a cold breath on the back of his neck, remembering all the things he had heard about this man Griff Jordan. His incredible luck, for one thing. Keller, and fighting George Wheat, and now—Were Lawler and Macready dead? Or was one of them badly wounded and already talking about who'd paid for the ambush on Jordan? He thought of Lisa and what she would say. My God, it might be the end of them. She might go to Austin and never come back.

And then through the crowd discussing the shooting of Jordan, he saw Art Lawler. Lawler jerked his head in the lobby door and went out the hall toward the rear of the hotel and then to the alley. In a minute Benbow followed him out and heard the whole story.

Later, his face white, Benbow came back into the bar-room, his hand on Lawler's shoulder. With a heavy fist Benbow rapped on the bar for attention. "My man Macready's dead. Griff Jordan shot him."

"In self-defense, likely," a man far back in the crowd muttered. Benbow didn't even try to identify the speaker. "I sent Lawler and Macready over to the Goodrich place to see about leasing some land. They overheard Jordan and Goodrich talking. Well, Macready got so damned mad, and who can blame him, that he waited all night, him and Lawler, to jump Jordan."

"Mad about what?" somebody asked.

"Reckon there's few of us here who didn't lose kin in the war between the states."

"That's for certain!"

"What'd you think of a born Texan who went north to fight against his own brother?"

For a moment there was silence, then came a buzz of excited talk. "Who you talkin' about, Clyde?"

"You tell 'em, Art," Benbow said, turning to the man with the scarred mouth.

Without hesitation Lawler recounted how he had overheard Griff Jordan admit that he had fought for the North.

"Now I don't ask anybody to believe me or my men," Benbow said loudly into the confusion of voices that followed Lawler's statement. "So I suggest a bunch of us ride out to the Goodrich place and ask the old man. He may deny it, but we can tell by lookin' at him if he's hidin' anything."

This was accomplished before the afternoon was over. But Sheriff Sam Enright, who had done most of the questioning of old Mark Goodrich, and tricked him into an admission, also threw some doubt on Lawler's story of the gunfight. When they rode down to where Macready's body still sprawled over the rock, it didn't take much sign reading to tell that two men had been hiding in the rocks, waiting to 'bush a man riding down the trail.

Even though some of the crowd of horsemen stated that a damned turncoat should have his neck stretched on general principles, Enright rallied enough support to make his point.

"The war's over, boys," Enright said. "If you don't want Jordan around there's other ways of getting rid of him."

On the way back to town Benbow gradually lost some of the resentment he had been holding against the sheriff. Things might work out all right, after all. He was thinking of the exact wording the Chainlink rider had used when he summoned Purcell to the ranch: "*Jordan's right arm's been shot to rags.*" It *was* the right arm, wasn't it? Benbow carefully reviewed the terse statement. Yes, it was the right arm. A slow smile crept across his face.

It was dark when he got back to town and went to the house. Lisa was in her room. When he knocked on her door he intended telling her about Jordan. Then, as he heard her steps coming, he decided against it. Let her find out for herself. And she would. The town was talking of nothing else.

She opened the door, and lamplight glowed behind her. "Yes, Clyde?"

"I just want you to know I didn't get a chance to see Jordan today. But I'll have that talk with him—" He reached through the door, widening it a little so that he could take her hands in his. He saw her nightdress with the rosebuds about the throat, saw the way it was cut in at the waist and all the rest of it. His teeth clenched and his jaw muscles showed ribbed and white beneath the weathered skin of his face.

She was frightened a little for she had never seen him like this. "Clyde, what is it?"

"You don't love him, do you?"

She sensed she must be very careful. But still she must be fair to herself. "I hardly know him, Clyde."

"I hope you won't know him any better," he said and gave her a fierce smile. Then he leaned forward and did something he had never done before. He kissed her on the mouth and she was so startled she just stood and looked at him.

"Sorry, Sis. But it's you and me against the world." The grin faded a little and he said in a softer voice, "Good night, Lisa."

"Good night, Clyde." And she quickly closed

the door and leaned against it. She wiped her mouth on the back of her hand. Her own brother!

And then through the door she heard him mutter as he turned away, "The right arm, by God. The right! Shot to rags!"

She had no idea at all what he had meant by that.

GRIFF opened his eyes and for a moment didn't realize he was lying in one of the bedrooms at Chainlink. He flexed his right arm and pain was a white hot wire into his brain. He closed his eyes, sweating, and heard a murmur of voices. It was dark. A lamp was lighted on the table and he saw magnified shadows against the 'dobe walls.

". . .. I'm going to wait the night through," Doc Purcell was saying in a low voice. "God knows I want to save the arm. But it's too early to tell."

"Don't take it off, Doc!" It was Ed Damon's voice pleading.

"Take it easy, Damon. I saw a lot of these wounds in the war. If this was a field hospital the arm would have come off immediately. But this is not war. We can afford to wait a little, to gamble."

"I got only one eye, Doc, but I can get around. But a man like Griff—Doc, they'd kill him. And with one arm he couldn't defend himself."

"I'd like to discuss this with the major."

"He—he's still sick."

"You mean drunk."

"Yeah—drunk." Damon sounded disgusted. He told how the major had got slicked up this morning as if intending to go to town. He'd emptied the whisky into a wash basin and thrown the empty bottle into the yard. And then he'd finished off the whisky anyway.

Griff lay in a cold sweat. His arm. His good right arm. He started to get up, but weakness claimed him. He'd lost blood, so much blood.

Ed Damon said, "How long till you'll know about the arm, Doc?"

"It's hard to say." The doctor sounded worried. "Just in case I have to amputate, get water on to heat. And find me all the clean cloths you can for bandages."

"You can't take off his arm, Doc!"

"You want him dead?"

Griff Jordan, his eyes bright with fever, got unsteadily to his feet still wearing his clothes. The two men whirled at the sound of him stomping into his boots.

"I thought you were asleep, Jordan." Purcell looked worried.

Griff showed his teeth. He lurched as if he were drunk. With his beaten face and the blood-soaked bandage he looked ghastly. "How much did Clyde Benbow pay you, Doc?"

Purcell's face flushed with anger. "That's an insult. You're a sick man, otherwise I'd—"

"Damn it, how much is he paying you to take off my arm?"

"Listen, Jordan. You were in the service. You know what gangrene is. Men die of it."

"Then I'll die," Griff Jordan said weakly. "I was born with two good arms. I'll die with two."

"I'm not certain I'll have to take your arm. Give me a little more time."

Griff jerked his gun rig off the back of a chair and asked Damon to buckle it on for him. But that was foolish, for he couldn't reach the holster. He got the gun loose and jammed it in his belt where he could reach the butt with his good left hand.

"Don't be a fool, Jordan!" Purcell cried.

Griff staggered out into the darkness, Damon at his heels. "Where you goin', Griff?" the one-eyed segundo asked anxiously.

174

"To hell if I have to." He lurched across the yard to a saddled horse and Damon gave him a boost into the seat.

When Griff reined away and put a spur to the horse, Purcell came running up. "Go after him, Damon."

"He'll kill the man that tries to get him. I know Griff pretty well."

"Then trail him," the doctor said, panting, staring off into the darkness where Jordan had vanished.

"I'll see that he gets where he's goin'," Damon said. "Wherever that is." And he ran for a horse.

Griff slowed his horse and began to shout at the darkness. "I'm not letting your Clyde Benbow see me one-armed and then laugh and shoot the buttons off my shirt! Not this boy, Doc! Not this boy!"

In a few more minutes Griff Jordan had convinced himself he was whole again. He didn't know where he was. He didn't know what time it was and he dared not throw back his head and look up at the stars for fear of losing his balance.

He looked carefully around and saw a distant

twinkle of lights and set the horse in that direction. Several times he roused himself to find the black horse he rode standing still. He clucked it into movement again.

Well, this time he'd settle with Clyde Benbow. And with Art Lawler at the same time. He knew that Benbow had paid for the ambush that very nearly had cost him his life.

He'd kill Benbow. Too bad a man like that had any kinfolks left to mourn him. Especially bad when the kin was a pretty girl like Lisa.

But it couldn't be helped. Benbow was the sort who was born to die violently. And die he would. He realized finally that it was dawn. It was very warm. And the pain now was dull against a bruised place far back in his mind.

He came to some greenery and saw ahead the flat-roofed buildings of Del Carmen. A grin crossed his lips, more of a grimace than a grin. It would soon be over, he told himself. He'd finish Benbow and then he'd take care of Mr. Art Lawler.

Ahead he saw a freighter pulling out, heading east, big wheels dripping dust, oxen moving with their stolid strength against harness. He could dimly hear the crack of a bullwhip and hear the shout of the teamster.

Because even his fevered brain recognized danger, Griff kept to the trees so as to come up on the main part of Del Carmen through the cottonwoods. It was when he entered the sparse shade offered by scraggly trees that he suddenly found himself peering straight up at the sky.

A semblance of sanity returned with a rush of cold fear as he realized he had tumbled from the saddle. But his right foot was still in the stirrup.

He saw that only his shoulders and the back of his head touched the ground. With his left hand he was clinging to the leather of the monkey-nosed tapadero. Beside him a trembling black horse was wheeling and snorting. Through the thin fabric of his much-washed shirt he could feel the uneven ground slide under his shoulders as he was slowly being dragged.

If that horse started to run—

"Easy," he said hoarsely. "Easy—" He tried to calm the horse but it pivoted, throwing up its head, eyes wild. Dragging him a little faster now. Walking still, not running. But at any moment the hoofs might flash and an iron shoe crush his skull.

"Easy—"

He felt the gathering of the black's muscles and then came a light step and he saw skirts swinging about pale white legs. He felt the horse quiet down and then a woman's voice: "Try and get your foot free. I'll hold him."

But because of his injured arm he could not free himself and in his efforts he fell back, his head crashing against the ground. When he regained his senses he saw that his foot was freed and the black horse tied to a cottonwood.

Maydelle Ashley came to stare down at him. "You've been bad hurt." She knelt beside him. "I've heard talk. Lawler or Macready shot you."

"So you know."

"Talk's all over town. You're an outcast, just like me, Griff Jordan."

"Outcast?"

"I'm what I am and you're a turncoat."

He looked up at her, his face rigid. And with his bad arm he never felt so helpless in his life. "How did you know?" he managed to gasp.

"They made old man Goodrich tell."

He saw now that she seemed much younger than at their first meeting when she'd been washing her hair in the yard and he had given her the thousand dollars to go away with.

Which she hadn't done, of course. Now he was glad she had stayed.

"Marge, Vickie," Maydelle suddenly shouted. "Come give me a hand."

He tried to get up, but he was weak. So goddam weak he couldn't tear paper. Two girls came out of the big two-story house he could see through the trees. The black-haired one had been at the door the first night he had tried to see the niece of Major Milo Clay.

The other was redheaded. Between the three of them they got him to his feet and walked him to the house and up a flight of narrow stairs and to an attic room where there was a cot and a narrow window.

When the other two girls had gone Maydelle said, "I'll help you off with your clothes." When he held back she shook her head and gave him a sad smile. "Look, just pretend I'm a nurse. You're a sick man and you need a nurse."

When his clothes were hanging over the back of a chair, she put a fresh bandage on his arm. She went out and returned later with a hot brew. "Yerba buena tea" she said, and sat on the edge of the cot and held a cup to his lips. "It'll cure anything. The Mexicans swear by it.

Mama Maria used to—" Her voice broke, and she looked down at the floor. "A woman I used to live with said it'll cure anything."

"You mean Maria Goodrich. I hear they raised you."

She got up, her face tight. "You're not very popular in this town right now, Jordan. There's men who, if they got drunk enough, might hang you. So you lie quiet and don't go talkin' about things that are over and done with."

"Old man Goodrich told me his wife loved you like her own daughter."

"But I had a baby, Mr. Jordan. And I was suddenly the wickedest thing that ever walked."

"Nothing wicked about you then. It was Clyde Benbow—"

"Don't say nothin' about Clyde."

"You still love him?"

"I'm tryin' hard not to." She looked him over, his face bruised from the fist fight, his right arm bandaged and in a sling. In his eyes she saw the fires of fever.

"Get word to your uncle at Chainlink." His voice was failing. "He'll come and get us both—"

"I told you once that I got no uncle. If you

don't like it here, if you're too good to hide in a cat house—"

"Maydelle." He caught her hand. His own was hot as fire. She looked worried.

"You can't leave here, Jordan. The least that'll happen is they'll brush you with hot tar and feather you with somebody's old mattress."

He fell asleep and she stood watching him a moment. Then she turned and cupped the lamp chimney and blew out the flame. Before she left the room she looked back. Yes, she thought, maybe here was somebody who could make her forget Clyde Benbow ever lived. Two of a kind they were. Outcasts. Maybe. Just maybe . . .

She tiptoed out and closed the door.

Only Ed Damon, the one-eyed segundo, knew where Jordan had gone. He had trailed his horse that night. But he told everybody else he had lost the trail. The story got around that Griff Jordan had gone to Mexico. But Ed Damon waited. He knew Griff Jordan would come back. Back with a good right arm. It had to be that way. It wasn't right for the man to be crippled.

181

14

I T took Griff Jordan ten days to throw off the fever. He came to his senses one night with the bedclothes soaked from his own perspiration. When he tried to sit up he was so weak the pain exploded in his brain and he had to lie back down. For a moment a terrible fear assailed him that his arm was gone. But when he felt of it he knew it was still a part of him. Maydelle cooked his meals and spoon-fed him until he was able to sit up. He thought the house seemed unusually quiet for such an enterprise, but he said nothing.

He didn't know that the town was surprised because the two girls formerly associated with Maydelle Ashley had cleaned out a deserted house north of town and there started their own operation. When questioned as to why Maydelle had suddenly closed her doors, they refused to discuss it.

Besides locking the doors Maydelle had covered the lower floor windows. Doc Purcell was worried about her, holding that with sin or without it, a human being deserved whatever help a doctor could give. Thinking she might be ill, Doc drove out, but Maydelle shouted from an upstairs window that she had never felt better and had no need for his pills.

Peering up from his buggy seat, Purcell was thinking that she really did look better than he could remember. She wore no lip rouge and her face seemed younger and her eyes had a sparkle.

Shaking his head, he drove back to the livery stable. Being a man of experience, he realized that only two things could bring about such a change in a woman like Maydelle. Either she had got religion or she had found a man.

The day Griff tried his legs he realized he had forgotten how to use them. But after several tries he managed to walk after a fashion. Maydelle watched him, a half smile on her lips. Down the attic steps in the big quiet house, she left her bedroom door open.

"You'll get your strength back, Griff," she said one morning and gave him a long look. "You're probably strong enough—for most things right now."

That bothered him almost as much as the secretive smile she would give him from time to time. The first he learned of her new virtue was when she made an off-hand remark that her doors were closed. Forever, she said.

"And I mean it, Griff, you'll see. A person can change."

"I'm glad, Maydelle."

"I was a stupid fool to think I could hurt Clyde by—by doing what I did."

He ate the noon meal of boiled beef and potatoes and some greens. When it was over he tried to roll a cigarette but the fingers of his right hand still didn't work right and he felt the beginnings of a small fear. To be without the use of his right hand a man might as well be dead. . . .

She knelt beside his chair and rolled the cigarette and put it between his lips and lighted it for him.

"Tonight, Griff?" she whispered, and ran her hands along his thick left arm. "Tonight."

She turned away and climbed the stairs with a lamp in her hand. Later, when he passed down the hall on his way to the attic he saw her door open. But he went on up to his own quarters.

She came to him then, the moonlight spilling through the window to put gold on her flesh and upon the long hair streaming down her naked back.

"Why, Griff?" she demanded in a low, hurt voice.

"Why what?"

"Is it because—because of what I did before? Can't you touch me because of that? Can't you put your hands on me?"

He sat up on the cot. "Maydelle, I appreciate what you did for me, but—"

"Appreciate!" She came close, her hands clenched against the tight flesh of her thighs. "When you were sick, you told me you loved me. You said you'd looked a long time for a woman, but now you'd found her."

"I said that?"

"I thought you meant me! Was it somebody else you meant?"

He shook his head in bewilderment. He knew he might not be able to cope with her in his present condition. He saw the edge of hysteria in her eyes. He could sense it too, in the way her breasts rose with her ragged breathing.

"Who was this woman, Griff?" she demanded. "If it wasn't me?"

Suddenly he remembered what he had said in his fevered ravings. "Lisa Benbow."

Maydelle fled the room and in a moment she returned, a wrapper belted tight about her enraged body. "Get out, Griff!" she screamed. "Get the hell out of my house!"

He got up then, unsteadily, and caught her by the wrists and threw her across the cot and held her. "Listen to me!" His own weakness was curdling into a strong anger. "You're not the first person in the world who's been hurt!"

"I had a baby when I was just a kid—"

"Other people have had worse." He leaned close. "My God-fearing grandfather brought slaves to this country, Maydelle. In chains. In the filthy, rotten holds of his ships. You were in chains when you went with Clyde Benbow."

"I loved him. He said we'd marry."

"Is that any reason to end up like this? Putting yourself on the block. Making yourself a slave. You had a choice. The black men my illustrious grandfather brought here had no choice!"

"You a preacher or something?"

"I'm trying to make you realize that you can't hate the world because you had a baby. A lot of people tried to help you. The Goodriches. Your uncle—"

"I got no uncle."

186

"He's Sam Kinsfather. That was your mother's name."

"How d'you know? He ever tell you?"

"I've put a lot of things together. It doesn't make a pretty picture. But he's trying to undo the wrongs. He blames himself for what's happening to you."

She was weeping, watching him through the spread fingers of the hands she held over her eyes. "I s'pose after all he's done I'm to forgive—"

"Try it. You had a baby, it died. Forget Clyde Benbow."

She dried her eyes on the hem of the robe. "I almost forgot him, Jordan. Almost." Her bloodshot eyes were narrowed against his face. "Almost."

"Come to Chainlink with me."

"You can make me?"

"I'll tie you across a saddle if I have to."

She dried the tears off her face and grew silent. In the distance could be heard the rattle of a wagon. There was a hammering on the door downstairs and somebody saying drunkenly, "I told you the place is closed up!" Then steps fading in the darkness.

"You'll be well off, Maydelle," Griff said

earnestly. "Better off than anybody else here. Do you understand what that means?"

"I dunno."

"You've got to be strong to get along in this world. Believe me, I know. Forgive your uncle."

He talked on and his voice grew hoarse. At last he stepped back and she got up from the cot and pushed back her loose hair that had fallen over her shoulders when he handled her so roughly.

"All right," she said, and the hardness was back in her eyes. "I'll go to Chainlink with you."

"Good." He managed to smile at her.

She went to the door and looked back. "You done a lot of preachin' to me, Jordan. You said it takes a strong person to survive. You said I was weak because when Clyde wouldn't marry me I crawled through the mud."

"It does take strength."

"When you was outa your head, you done some wild talkin'. You said if you lost your arm you'd kill yourself. That's bein' real strong, ain't it, Mister Jordan?"

He shook his head and sighed. "I guess that's

the trouble with preaching sometimes. It's always for the other fellow. Not yourself."

In the morning she saddled the black horse that had been kept in the barn behind the big house, and rode to the stable and hired a wagon. He was waiting when she drove back, the black horse tied to the tailgate. When he asked why she hadn't packed a trunk, she said she wanted nothing from this place. Only the clothes on her back. These she'd burn, "if my generous uncle is goin' to lay out gold like you say."

People on the walks turned to stare and to speculate when Griff Jordan came along the street in a livery wagon. Maydelle was driving. He told her to pull up in front of a shop with its sign, *J. Edelmann, Gunsmith.*

Griff told the small, wiry little man what he wanted. "A scattergun."

"That's for a saloon. You going into that business?"

"I'm in the business of staying alive."

Edelmann licked his lips and laid out two shotguns on the counter. Griff tested the action of each weapon. He selected one and told Edelmann to cut the barrels down. He waited while this was done. In the meantime a crowd began to grow in the street outside the shop and Griff heard angry murmurs and ugly words: "Traitor —turncoat."

Leaving Maydelle in the wagon, he crossed over to the Del Carmen House. He carried the sawed-off shotgun under his good left arm. Doc Purcell, standing at the bar, murmured, when he saw Griff, "The second miracle of Del Carmen."

Griff nodded to the doctor. "I've still got my arm."

"You're a lucky man." Purcell came close, while those in the bar looked on angrily. "Im not going to improve my standing any by talking to you, but I have a certain warning to impart. The other day it suddenly occurred to me where you might be hiding out. I think Clyde Benbow has had the same idea. I've seen him watching the Ashley house—"

Then Benbow's voice crackled through the room: "I thought I smelled dead cat in here."

Griff turned, staring at Benbow, looming tall in the doorway. "Just the man I want to see," Griff said.

Benbow came farther into the room, the crowd parting, fear and anticipation beginning to bloom on many faces. "A man couldn't pick a better place to hide out," Benbow said with a grin. "Whisky and grub and about anything else that takes his fancy—" Then he saw the shotgun for the first time. He stood stiffly and there was a wariness now in his eyes.

"One of your men put a bullet in my right arm," Griff said. "But I can still use a shotgun."

"There isn't enough range in that buckshot to touch a man with a rifle," Benbow said, some of his ease returning.

"That's the only way you'll get me. With a rifle."

"I can throw a handful of sand farther than you can shoot that thing."

"It's made for close, belly-ripping work. I'd like to use it on you, Benbow."

"Turncoat."

"You won't try for me up close." Griff's eyes traveled slowly around the room. "None of you have the guts to try for me up close."

"No man's fool enough to buck a scatter-gun," Benbow said.

"I'll get my right hand working again. If not, then I'll practice with my left. When I'm ready I'll come after you, Benbow. Without the shotgun." He walked to the door, then looked back. "Maydelle Ashley is going out to Chain-link to live and—"

Benbow went white. "I won't have that whore living in the house where my sister was born—"

Griff lifted the shotgun and Purcell cried: "No, Jordan! They'll hang you sure!"

Griff halted, realizing how close he had come to sending a charge of buckshot into Benbow's face. And Benbow seemed to realize how close he had come to death, for his body was braced instinctively as if to take the full shock of the blast from those twin barrels.

Griff said, "When Miss Ashley comes to town, she's to be treated like a lady." He looked around, then at Benbow, whose face was slick with sweat. "Benbow, tell your friend Lawler better luck next time."

Then he was gone. The crowd moved to the hotel porch and watched Maydelle, a feather in her hat, drive the wagon out of town. Griff Jordan sat stiffly on the seat beside her, the shotgun in his lap.

"I'll say this," a man said hoarsely, "Jordan's got guts."

"And they'll be showing one of these days," Benbow said through his teeth.

He bulled his way through the crowd and to the big house and there he found Lisa doing needlepoint in the parlor. She seemed pale and drawn, and not at all her lively self. He had noted the change in her since the shooting of Griff Jordan and his disappearance.

"I just saw Jordan," he said, and saw the quick surprise, the flush, the dropping of the needlepoint as she jerked out of her chair.

"He's all right?"

"Yeah. Guess where he's been hiding?"

"It doesn't matter. To know that he's alive and well—"

"Hiding at Maydelle's place."

"Maydelle Ashley?" The color went out of her face.

"They drove out to Chainlink together."

"If she's been hiding him, I admire her for it."

"Hiding a damned turncoat, Lisa. A traitor to his own people."

A little frown rippled like a wave across her pale forehead, and then the tears came and she ran up the stairs to her room.

Benbow went out into the backyard to smoke a cigar and consider his next move. He decided he'd go have a talk with George Wheat. George must be getting restless down there in the shack along the river.

15

ONCE out of town Griff took over the reins from Maydelle. Although his right arm was still stiff there was no longer pain. Now he had to concentrate on strengthening it. "You're starting a new life today," Griff told her. "Forget everything that's happened."

She sat hunched forward in the seat, hands gripping her knees through the thin fabric of her dress. "What if some of the Chainlink men laugh behind my back?"

"The man who laughs will get fired." He gave her a sidelong glance. "When I said to forget everything, I meant just that. It includes Clyde Benbow."

"I hate him," she said firmly.

As they approached Chainlink headquarters he saw the major come to the yard and shield his eyes against the sun. At least he appeared sober today and for that Griff gave his thanks. When they passed the bunkhouse he saw from the corner of his eye some of the men staring at Maydelle and then talking behind their hands. He knew this would never do. Already there was enough chaos at Chainlink. The revelation that he was a turncoat, the major's drunkenness, and now Maydelle Ashley. A woman like Lisa Benbow these men would respect. But how much respect would they offer Maydelle Ashley?

He drove up in front of the house and the major stood stiffly in the sun, wearing a vest, white shirt and dark pants. Although he seemed sober enough his face looked older and there was a puffiness around the eyes. This man, Griff thought, would die within the year if he didn't stop drinking. What the hell good would his money do him then?

Maydelle stepped down from the wagon and she and her uncle looked at each other for an embarrassed moment. Then Major Milo Clay hurried forward and put an arm about Maydelle's waist and said in a choked voice, "Welcome home."

She drew back a moment, staring at him. Then her face broke and she threw herself against his slight figure and sobbed. Griff drove down to the barn. One of the hands took the team.

Ed Damon, wiping his face on a bandanna, came up from the breaking corral. "Good to see you, Griff," the one-eyed segundo said.

"Good to see you," Griff said and looked around. "Good to be back."

"I knew where you was all the time, Griff. I kept an eye on you."

Griff gave him a friendly slap on the shoulder, then sobered as Damon gave him an embarrassed look. "How many of the hands drew their time when they heard about me fighting for the North?"

"Six. I tried to hire more, but a lot of the boys are gettin' scared out. They don't want to work for you, Griff. Besides that, they hear things are blowin' up bad between you an' Benbow. They don't want to get sucked into a range feud."

"And how do you feel, Ed? About the war, I mean?"

"I never fought on either side, Griff. And if I had, it wouldn't make a damn bit of difference."

Griff felt warmed. "When we cut up a few profits around here, Ed, you'll get your share."

Damon nodded toward the house where the

major and Maydelle were on the porch, talking. "How you think this'll work out, Griff?"

"We've got the world by the tail. I hope it doesn't get away from us."

"I hope we don't have trouble with her bein' here."

"Keep the men away from her."

"I'll do my damnedest. How's the arm, Griff?"

"I won't win any medals shooting with it."

That afternoon Griff had his gear moved from the main house to what had formerly been a harness shed. The earth floor was tamped and oiled and a cot and chest of drawers moved in.

At full dark Griff lay in his new quarters, staring at the rain-marked ceiling. Nothing— nothing would stop him, he vowed. This was his one last chance. As he clenched his fists he felt the stiffness in the fingers of his right hand. For the first time in his life he knew real fear. A man could bluff with a sawed-off shotgun. But what if an enemy tricked him into discharging both barrels? And then, before he could reload, emptied a pistol into him?

What would the day of his dying be? A day like today had been, with the sun bright in a clear sky? What would his final thoughts be? Would there be time to think at all? . . .

The next morning he had his talk with the major, suggesting he take Maydelle and travel for a time. Or at least go to San Antone or perhaps Austin. "You'll be surprised," Griff went on, "what short memories folks have if you bring her back wearing fancy clothes and showing all the evidences of your wealth."

"The same old story, eh, Griff?" the major said with a bitter laugh. "People love money and power. The rich man sins and they laugh politely. The poor man sins and they look for a rope."

"Not quite as bad as that," Griff said. "But if we build this ranch into something, then Chainlink will earn the respect of our neighbors. Then in turn they'll learn to respect Maydelle."

"And how about respect for you, Griff?"

"I knew the risk I was running when I decided to throw in with you and come back here."

They were walking down by the corral. The hands were roping out their morning horses.

Griff said, "You've made your peace with Maydelle?"

"She says she's forgiven me. I only hope she means it."

That day the major and Maydelle took the livery wagon to Del Carmen. There they would take the stage which would take them eventually to San Antone where they planned to spend several months. Griff shook hands with the major and tipped his hat to Maydelle. She did not look at him.

"I owe you a lot, Maydelle," he said, "for taking care of me. I'll never forget it."

She didn't even look around. The major looked embarrassed and gave Griff a wan smile, then kicked off the brake and drove away. Griff had a hunch that the major's life with his niece would present its problems. But he had more important things to consider. There were wells to clean out, harness to mend, a constant lookout to keep for straying cattle.

When the major had driven off Ed Damon came up. "Figured to let you get settled a mite before springin' the bad news."

"Trouble?" Griff asked.

"We been losin' cows. Tracks lead toward the border. I can see where they've been pushed across the river, but there ain't a trace the other side of the line."

The next day Griff took some men and went south into the Chisos mountains, following the trail of the stolen cattle. According to the sign, this latest bunch of about ten head was being hazed along by three riders. But as Damon had said, the tracks faded the other side of the river. And neither could they find anyone who had seen a small bunch of cattle being pushed south. "*No comprendo*," was all he could get out of the border Mexicans who believed the way to a long life was to profess ignorance on all subjects.

The summer seared the grass and Griff saw creeks dry up and water holes become mud sinks. They lost cattle from the drought. But then they got a rain. The rustlers, whoever they were, kept away from the Chainlink herd. Griff went to New Mexico during the fall and hired more men, riders who didn't give a damn which side a man had fought on during the war. On Griff's orders no Chainlink hand ever rode out of headquarters without belt loops filled with shells, a holstered revolver and a booted rifle. But there was no trouble.

Benbow left him alone and this worried him. Better that Benbow would come into the open. According to range gossip Benbow was stocking the sections he had leased from old man Goodrich. Nobody questioned the source of his money now. He was spending it and the merchants of Del Carmen were happy.

Only at night when he lay alone in his quarters did Griff think of Lisa. He had not seen her since the day of the fight with George Wheat.

Fall blended into winter and they had blue northers in January when the cold knifed through fleece-lined jackets as if you were wearing burlap. Griff made only two trips to town that winter, his sawed-off shotgun under his arm.

The looks he received from the citizens would have driven out a lesser man. But Griff, as he moved along the walks, looked straight ahead. He heard the muttered oaths behind his back. Once when he, by force of habit, entered the bar at the Del Carmen House, he saw the sign above the backbar: *No Turncoats Wanted*. And saw the cold stares of the patrons.

Abruptly he turned his back and went out. At the West Texas Store, where he had come for supplies, he learned Chainlink no longer had credit. It was pay cash now "or take your business clear to Paso, for all we care," the clerk said. "Maybe they ain't so particular about doing business with a traitor."

The clerk was a small man and therefore felt himself secure from Griff Jordan's wrath. Jordan took a leather sack from his pocket, counted out the coins to pay for his merchandise and then loaded the wagon himself.

He was taking a shortcut across a weed-grown lot when the door to a cottage opened and Doc Purcell beckoned to him. Griff tied the team and went in. Purcell said he had just put on a pot of coffee and Griff was welcome.

"I'm a little surprised at this courtesy," Griff said.

Purcell shrugged. "I like a man for what he is. Not what he was. It's the present that counts. Now, today." He banged a fist on the kitchen table where they were taking their coffee. "If only the fool human race could realize it."

Because he felt he should explain to this man who was trying to be friendly, Griff told why he had fought for the North.

Purcell nodded. "It took guts to come back to Texas. I sensed your problem the night we had our talk at Chainlink."

"A man can't run. It took me ten years to realize that."

"I hear the major is wintering in San Antone with his niece."

Griff nodded. Whenever he thought of Milo Clay living the gay life, he felt a slow resentment. The major had sent no money for salaries and Griff had been forced to deplete their meager supply of cash.

"I suppose you know that Lisa Benbow is living in Austin," Purcell said.

Griff felt his heart leap, but kept his voice casual. "That so?" No wonder he hadn't seen her around town.

"Talk is that she's going to marry a man in the freighting business there."

Griff was barely able to conceal his surprise and hurt. He finished his coffee. "I wish her happiness," he said.

Purcell put down his cup. "A doctor sometimes develops an insight, after a fashion. I sense how you feel about her."

"I only saw her a few times."

"And I sense she feels the same way about you." He leaned forward. "If you could explain the way you did to me. About fighting for the

North. I'm sure she'd understand. Lisa is a fine person."

"So that's why she went to Austin." Griff felt his lips stiffen. "I've got a ranch to run, Doc. I can't go traipsing to Austin."

"You could write. I have her address."

"No thanks, Doc."

"Few people around here understand a man with an ideal. Lisa would understand."

"She was apparently willing enough to believe the worst of me," Griff said.

"Why didn't you ride in and explain when you first heard the story was out?"

"What difference would it have made?"

"You love her, don't you?"

The question was so sudden, so devastating, that Griff clenched his hands and turned to stare out the window at the haze of smoke from cook fires that lay above the town. "Yes, damn it, I love her."

As he was driving out of town the sounds of an approaching horse caused him to halt the wagon and reach for his shotgun. It was Sheriff Sam Enright who rode up. "Have you or the major ever heard from Leithbut?"

"Not a word. Don't see why he should write, though."

"Leithbut sorta dropped off the face of the earth." The sheriff looked grim for a moment. "One thing you hate about a job like this is the fact that one day you might have to hang a man. A man you used to ride with, a man you watched grow up. A man with a fine sister who'd have her heart busted right down the middle if that happened."

"You mean Clyde Benbow, I take it."

"Didn't mention any names, did I?" The sheriff reined his horse away from the wagon. "Watch yourself, Jordan. Benbow's been too quiet lately to suit me."

"Thanks for the warning, but why? I'm still a turncoat."

"You ain't the only Texan that fought North."

Griff's mouth opened. "You'd lose that job quick if anybody around here knew that."

"If you say anything I'll deny it." Enright leaned over the horn. "Durin' the war a lot of fellas drifted outa here. They didn't come back for a long time. Then they drifted back. A man wasn't beholden to say where he'd been."

Thoughtfully Griff drove on down the road, hardly aware that the team, of their own accord, took the turnoff that led to Chainlink.

206

16

O N the day Griff spotted the first blade of spring grass he knew it was time to plan roundup. That night he and Ed Damon discussed the project. But Griff had no heart for it. He knew why: Lisa Benbow.

That week he received a letter from the major. He was feeling poorly, the major said, but Maydelle seemed to have blossomed out in San Antone where she was unknown. *If there's any one thing I ever did in this world, Griff,* the major wrote, *it's saving that girl.* But the major made no mention of Chainlink. Apparently he had lost all interest in the ranch.

However, there was a postscript: *By the way, we ran into Lisa Benbow. Down here from Austin on a visit. It was quite a surprise. She seems to have lost her sparkle. After a few moments of embarrassment she and Maydelle seemed to forget all the ugliness and began to talk about the old days. It was quite a refreshing afternoon. Lisa inquired as to your health.*

Keep up the good work, Griff. When I'm feeling better we'll be home.

Slowly Griff folded the letter. *So she asked about me*, he thought dully.

Two days later Griff was taking the morning meal with the crew when Ed Damon, who had been making a spot check of the nearest bunches of Chainlink beef, rode in on a winded horse. While the crew gathered around tensely, Damon revealed that he had struck sign where about two hundred head had been run off.

Griff swore softly. In the business of raising beef in West Texas a man had to be prepared to lose a few head, such as the bunches that had been run off before. But two hundred head —"That's going too damned far, Ed."

The trail led south and east, crossing Median Creek, Damon said.

Later, Griff rode out with eight men, leaving Damon at headquarters. Because the Goodrich home place was only a few miles from where Damon saw the rustler sign at Median Creek, Griff led his men that way.

Goodrich seemed ill-at-ease. "Reckon you think I double-crossed you, Griff, by tellin' that you was the son of Bullhide Jordan."

"No. I heard how it happened." He and

Goodrich were in the kitchen. Griff's men were lounging in the shade of the barn. He told Goodrich of his letters from the major. He'd ridden out of his way a little so as to tell the old man how Maydelle was getting along. But he didn't seem pleased.

Goodrich studied the backs of his blue-veined hands. "She the same as killed my wife. Her and Clyde."

Griff leaned across the table. "Speaking of Clyde, I've missed some beef. Little bunches that I trailed into Mexico. But now they're starting to really hit Chainlink."

Goodrich smiled for the first time since Griff's arrival. "When you find Clyde Benbow, hang him."

"I'd rather take him in and let the sheriff handle it."

"I want to live just long enough to see that bastard dropped off the back of a horse with a rope collar around his neck."

"I could shoot him, maybe." Griff stared out the window where Miguel, the Goodrich vaquero, was lugging harness to the barn. "Hang him, no."

"It's on account of Lisa, ain't it?"

"Maybe." Griff tried to sound indifferent.

"Clyde ain't her real brother."

Griff straightened up in the chair. "You're joking."

"I'll swear on Maria's grave," Goodrich said. "Even Lisa didn't know it. I wrote the girl and told her the truth. Likely she didn't believe me."

"Not her brother?" Griff sounded incredulous. "I just can't believe it."

"Let me tell you something, Griff. I'm the only one left around here that remembers when old man Benbow come to this country. That was more'n thirty year back. The old man was disappointed in his first-born, Tom. Tom didn't have no fire like the old man. And one day the old man found a two-year-old kid down on the river. Somebody had turned him out. God knows who. But the old man took him home and made his wife and Tom swear they'd never let on that the kid wasn't their own."

"Then how did you find out about it?"

"I was with the old man the day he found Clyde."

"How about Clyde? Does he know?"

"Sure he knows. He knew there was somethin' to his life before he come to Chainlink. He kept pesterin' old Benbow and finally the old man told him. The old man was fed up with Clyde by that time. He found out Clyde had been stealin' Chainlink hosses and sellin' 'em across the line."

Griff shook his head. "Lisa thinks he's her brother. I couldn't hang him. And even if she learned the truth, she must have some feeling for him. Bad as he is. They were raised together."

"She's the only human on earth Clyde's got any use for. Reckon he's been in love with her since she was a kid."

"Maybe it's better that she's gone from here," Griff said. "Better that she's going to be married."

"I didn't know she was fixin' to take herself a husband," Goodrich said in surprise.

Because Miguel Aleman knew the wild land across the river as most men know the palms of their hands, the Goodrich vaquero rode out with them. Along the old Comanche trail they moved, through the rough country of the Chisos. Griff saw brush trampled on either side of the steep trail where the two hundred head had been pushed fast.

At last they came to the Rio and rode down into the willows. Miguel Aleman swam his

211

horse across and went to make inquiries among the numerous relatives he had who resided along the river.

While he was gone Griff impatiently paced the river bank. Occasionally he would look across at the broken country that was Mexico. A man could spend a year down there hunting stolen cattle. And in the meantime Chainlink would go to seed. He felt a slow unreasoning anger that the major was off having himself a time with his niece, while the burdens of Chainlink rested on the shoulders of Griffith Jordan. Then he forced out the mood of self-pity. After all, the major had given him this chance for a future. The major wouldn't be the first man to leave the dull and sometimes dangerous business of running a ranch in the hands of a ramrod-partner.

Shortly before sundown Miguel Aleman came back dripping water from the river crossing. The cattle trail was plain across the river, he said, flinging out a brown hand in that direction. But eight, maybe nine miles south there was a canyon. In the canyon two hundred head of beef grazed. And in the rocks were some twenty men all heavily armed. It was unmistakably an ambush.

Griff swore softly. He'd had one sample of a Benbow ambush the day Lawler and Macready tried to finish him.

He gave the matter only a moment's thought. They could ride down there and make a fight of it, even though they were outnumbered two to one. But to win they'd have to be damned lucky.

Looking around the circle of tense faces that awaited his orders, he knew many of these men would never come back. And for what? Two hundred head of beef. And the major didn't even give a damn whether it was two hundred or two thousand.

Griff pounded his forehead with the heel of his hand. Why was the fact that Milo Clay was enjoying himself in San Antone so irritating? Well, there was no use turning his back on the problem. It was a very real one. He resented the major's complete lack of cooperation. Griff had written him that the men had not been paid for a month. The major in his last letter had not even mentioned the matter.

Griff tightened his cinch. "We're going home," he told the men. It was bad enough to risk lives when you were paying your men their salaries on schedule.

They rode slowly north, back through the Chisos. This matter of the stolen beef would have to be settled on a personal basis. He'd ride in and have it out with Benbow. He flexed the stiffened fingers of his right hand. If it came to gunfire, then it would have to be that way. For a month now he had been practicing with his revolver.

He could still draw and fire. But whatever ability he might once have enjoyed had been lost the day Lawler sent that rifle slug tearing into his arm.

17

ON the day following Griff's long trip to the river, excitement swept Del Carmen. The bodies of Leithbut and the Oakum brothers, hired on as bodyguards, had been found at the edge of the Davis Mountains. Also the remains of a team shot to death and a burned wagon. The discovery had been made by a cowhand for the Turkey Track outfit. Even though the bodies were badly decomposed it was plain to see that they had been scalped.

Comanches!

Men gathered in groups along the street, talking in hushed tones. Three times, while this part of the country was growing, the Comanches had forced the land to be abandoned. Even though the killings had obviously taken place months ago, it still caused alarm.

Clyde Benbow didn't hear of the discovery because he was many miles south, approaching a shack deep in the badlands near the river. The shack was made of slabs of shale piled one upon the other without benefit of masonry. The roof, made of willow poles, was plastered with mud.

As he approached he saw no sign of life. But as he reached the shack he could see, some distance away, a saddler in a crude corral partially screened by the willows.

George Wheat's voice reached him from some rocks. Benbow turned in the saddle and saw the giant come out from behind a boulder, rifle in his big hands. The backs of the hands were scarred, as was his face, from the battle with Griff Jordan.

"Next time whistle when you come up," Wheat said.

They went into the shack and Benbow handed over a bottle he had brought out from town.

Wheat sat down at a rickety table and slopped the liquor into a tomato can he used for a cup. He drained off the whisky, wiped his mouth on a hair-backed hand. "I'm gettin' sick of this, Clyde."

"Only a little longer, George." Benbow helped himself to some of the whisky.

"You're livin' high off the hog in town. I set down here an'—"

"Aren't we celebrating the finish of Griff Jordan?"

Wheat gave a harsh laugh. "That bastard. We had it fixed purty. But he got smarted up. Don't ask me how. We waited all day in that canyon with the sun bakin' our brains. He never come. Later we went to the river and seen where he turned back."

Benbow tried to hide his disappointment. "We'll try again."

"I been months down here," Wheat grumbled. "You told me you'd have Jordan buried by this time. We'd be back at Chainlink and I'd be your foreman—"

"It's on account of Lisa," Benbow said, trying to hold his irritation in check. "She doesn't want trouble. That's why I wanted Jordan to get killed in Mexico. It would have been better for me—"

"When's she comin' home?" George Wheat said, an old familiar hunger back in his yellow eyes.

"She'll get tired of Austin," Benbow said. "She'll come home if I have to go and get her." Benbow was leaning against a rusted stove. The only other furnishings were cut down barrels for seats and a double bunk piled high with filthy blankets.

"But when she does come back," Benbow said thinly, "you be sure and keep your feeling for her the faithful dog kind."

Wheat had been drinking from the tomato can. Now he lowered it. "She's the finest woman that ever lived. I wouldn't do nothin' to hurt her."

Benbow changed the subject. He told Wheat to get set for another try at Chainlink beef. There were always renegades across the river who'd do any job if paid enough. This bunch they'd been hiring to run off the Chainlink beef were being paid not only in newly-minted coins but by being allowed to sell the cattle they had rustled.

"Where's Lawler?" Benbow asked.

"Hangin' around a cantina across the river."

"Tell him to get the crew together. This time move off as much Chainlink stuff as you can. You and Lawler oughta be right happy to see Griff planted across the line."

"Yeah. But I don't hanker to have his sawed-off shotgun spittin' my brains out."

"I hear he doesn't carry it any more."

They discussed the rustling of Chainlink cows

at some length. Wheat always steered the conversation back to "I'm gettin' tired stayin' down here, Clyde. I want to go to town and—"

"You've got to keep out of sight for a spell."

"This is a damn long spell," Wheat said harshly.

"Sam Enright is nosing around too much to suit me."

Wheat stared at the bottle he held in his large hands. "I get a cold breath around my neck every time I think of a sheriff."

"He won't bother us if we just play the cards smart."

"Maybe we oughta dig up that money and light out."

"No."

Wheat set the bottle down carefully on the scarred top of the table. "You never did tell me where you hid that money, Clyde."

"Just give me time."

"You said I was your partner. I got a right to know. What if somethin' happens to you?"

"Then you'll be no worse off than you ever were," Benbow said through his teeth. "Broke. You were always broke."

Wheat got up, his yellow eyes flaming with anger. Benbow, a hand on his gun, wondered if now was as good a time as any to eliminate this "partner" for good.

"I helped you get that money," Wheat said ominously. "I got my rights. You said I'd be your partner at Chainlink. A ramrod-partner like Jordan is to the major."

"George, I'm not going to take much more off you. I'm running this show. I'll tell you when to sit up and when to bark—"

"Don't call me no dog, Clyde. Don't never do that! I'm a rich man. I'm rich as you. I could marry me a fine lady like your sister if I was a mind—"

A flag of red whipped behind Benbow's eyes and he almost drew his gun and killed George Wheat for even entertaining such a thought. But through one of the two windows in the shack he saw a rider some distance away on a ridge.

Wheat, seeing the intent look on Benbow's face, spun. For several minutes they watched the rider approach and pull up some fifty yards away. It was the sheriff. Benbow looked puzzled and worried.

The sheriff was calling, "Clyde! You in there?" sitting his horse fifty yards away, hunched over in the saddle, peering at the shack.

"He knows you're here," Wheat said tensely. "You let him trail you here."

"Sit tight," Benbow said. "I'll get rid of him."

Benbow went outside and got his horse and swung into the saddle, trying to make every move leisurely as if his conscience was as clear as one of the sand pools down on the river.

"Hi, Sam," Benbow said when he reined in where the sheriff was waiting. "What you doing way down here?"

"I might ask you the same, Clyde." The eyes in the sheriff's narrow face showed a polite inquiry.

"Lost some horses a few nights back," Benbow said. "Rustlers. I followed sign down here."

"Who's in the shack with you, Clyde?"

"Nobody. You better get some boys and go looking for those rustlers. It isn't the first time I've lost stock."

"They tell me Chainlink's been losing beef."

"Probably the same bunch."

"Might be Comanches," Enright said, and took a cigar from his pocket. Looping the reins over the saddle horn, he rolled the cigar between the palms of his hands.

Benbow laughed. "Comanches? Hell, we haven't seen any around here in quite a spell—"

The sheriff's bland manner vanished. He dropped the cigar he had been absently rolling. His gun came up, cocked. "Sit your saddle easy, Clyde," he warned. "Real easy."

Benbow stiffened and felt sweat break out from under his hat band. He sat with his back to the shale structure and he couldn't see George Wheat to signal that he needed help.

"What's the idea?" Benbow demanded. It was the only thing he could think to say. Where the hell was that stupid George Wheat? Still in the shack, likely. A man with a big body and a big skull, and nothing inside the skull but loco ideas about Lisa Benbow.

"This is the idea, Clyde," the sheriff said, his eyes cold. He told about the finding of Leithbut and the Oakum brothers. "Scalped. Some folks think it was Comanches."

Benbow put on his best poker face. "What you driving at?"

"Where'd you get all the money you been spending?"

"Chicago. Everybody knows that."

222

"Your lie has got threadbare, Clyde. I went through your things at the house in town."

"Your badge don't give you that right!"

"I found a letter that this Chicago outfit wrote. They said they'd back you in buyin' back Chainlink from Leithbut. They didn't say anything about you leasing land from Goodrich and stocking it—"

"That was in another letter." As he said it, Benbow realized how thin it sounded. "I burned that letter."

A taut smile flickered across Enright's lips. "Jordan claims the Leithbut wagon had eighty thousand dollars in it. Leithbut took the wagon over from the major. And him and the Oakum boys headed for Mexico along the old Davis road. They didn't quite make it."

"Look to Jordan," Benbow said, putting a sneer on his lips. "A damn turncoat like him would be the kind to kill Leithbut—"

"I looked in that old pair of boots you got in the house, Clyde." Benbow's eyes were murderous, but the sheriff, cocked revolver tight in his hand, pressed on. "There was most five thousand dollars hid in them boots. Fresh-minted gold. Where'd you hide the rest of it, Clyde?"

Benbow felt the seat of his saddle slick from his sweat. "That's money Poppa left me. I've been saving it."

The sheriff shook his head. "I was hoping this could be done before Lisa got home."

"Lisa's got nothing to do with this!"

"I know. But she's goin' to be almighty broke up when I hang you, Clyde. Just as I was pulling out this morning I saw her get off the stage."

Benbow looked sick. Cords tightened in his brown neck.

"I was heading over to the Goodrich place to talk to the old man," Enright went on, "when I seen you. I got real curious as to why you was ridin' down this way alone."

Rage added to the fear cocked Benbow's temper. "You should've brought some men with you, Sam!"

"I can handle you. I'm not afraid of you. Never have been. It's always been puzzlin' as to how a gentle woman like Mrs. Benbow could born you, Clyde. I don't remember your mother, but they say she was right nice. Reckon Tom and Lisa took after her. God knows who you took after—"

Benbow's hand had snapped down, but the

224

sheriff's voice caught him. "You can't make it, Clyde. A bullet from this gun will tear your guts all to hell. You've seen men die like that. So have I. It ain't pretty."

His face white, Benbow slowly lifted his right hand away from his gun.

"Now, Clyde, you tell whoever it is in that shack to come out. Tell 'em to make it fast. By the time I count three. Or you're a dead man. Real dead. One—"

Benbow's face was suddenly slick with sweat. "There's nobody in the shack, Sam."

"The hell there ain't. Two—"

Desperation gripped Benbow. Under pressure of the sheriff's gun George Wheat might talk. "Nobody's there, Sam. You don't see a horse, do you?"

"Tied off in the willows behind the place, maybe. Three—"

Benbow, his abdominal muscles contracted against the smash of the bullet from the sheriff's revolver, screamed, "George, come out! I'm covered!"

"So it was George Wheat," Enright breathed. "I figured as much. Now slide around easy with your left hand. Lift that gun and let it fall. I

225

can put three bullets in you before you can blink your eyes. And you know it."

The shot came suddenly from the rocks off to the sheriff's left side. But even before the crash of the rifle reached him, Benbow saw the sheriff slump forward across the horn, the side of his face shot away. His skittish horse, frightened by the shot, completed the job of unseating him.

Quickly Benbow stepped down and kicked away the sheriff's fallen revolver. Benbow was trembling. In a moment George Wheat came up, gripping a rifle. He was in his sock feet.

"I didn't think you could make it, George." Benbow's throat was so dry he could hardly talk.

"I went out the back window and snuck through the rocks. Scared Enright's hoss would get my scent." Wheat bent over the sheriff. "He dead?"

"You can see his brains, can't you?"

Benbow licked the sweat and fear off his lips. He peered south, toward Mexico. He could lose himself down there. Then he got a grip on his nerves.

"Killin' a sheriff ain't like gunnin' a cowhand," Wheat said, leaning on his rifle. "You reckon we can get away with it?"

"We *better* get away with it."

They stood in silence a moment, then Wheat said he was going to get his boots. His feet hurt. He put down the rifle and limped for the shack. Benbow knew now was the time to do it. If he was ever going to do it.

He picked up the rifle Wheat had laid aside and levered in a shell. The metallic sound caused Wheat to look around. He stood with his big body hunched, his gray socks full of burrs.

"I got me a Mex gal across the river, Clyde. Maybe some folks figure I'm stupid. But I give her a letter. If I don't come back, she'll see that it gets to some friends in Del Carmen. You savvy, boy? It tells everything we done together. Everything."

Benbow swallowed. "Go get your boots," he said easily. "I jacked a shell in this rifle just in case somebody heard the shot and come poking around."

Wheat went on to the shack. Sweating, Benbow rested the rifle butt against the ground. He didn't believe Wheat had a Mexican girl. Wheat was a dedicated man. In this world there was only one woman. Lisa. But he just might have done as he claimed. Sometimes the stupid showed an uncommon amount of cunning when you least expected it.

Wheat came out of the shack, wearing his boots. "I want my share of that dinero, Clyde. Now. Today."

Benbow knew argument was out now. For the present at least. He had to see how many others might believe as Sheriff Enright had, that Comanches didn't jump Leithbut and his wagon.

"We'll cover Enright's body with rocks," Benbow said. "Then we'll find us a couple of boys across the line who will swear they saw Griff Jordan do the killin'. Sound good?"

"Sounds good. Just let me be the one to pull the rope on Jordan."

"You do that. I'm going to be in town with Lisa."

Wheat showed his surprise. "You mean she's back?"

"Enright said she got back today."

They rode by the "Little Place" and picked up a pack mule. That afternoon, from the rear of a cave masked by brush where Benbow used to play as a boy, several canvas sacks were dug up. Wheat, his eyes glowing, took his share of the coins and rode out, leading the pack mule with its two weighted canvas sacks.

Again Benbow was tempted to finish it, by driving a bullet into the broad back. But he might need Wheat. He might need every man it was possible to call on, now that he sensed things were closing in on him.

18

WHEN Griff arrived back at Chainlink, tired and dusty from the long fruitless ride to the river, he was met by an excited Ed Damon. The one-eyed segundo handed him some mail that one of the riders had brought out from town. Then, his single eye twinkling, Damon said, "Miss Benbow was out here to see you."

Griff looked at him. "To see me? When?"

She'd come out that morning, Damon said. She'd be at the house in Del Carmen if he cared to call.

Griff's grin seemed broad as the Texas sky. "Get me a fresh horse saddled, Ed. I'll put on a clean shirt."

As he turned for his quarters Damon swung in beside him. "How'd you make out trailin' that rustled beef?"

Griff told Damon about the ambush that Miguel Aleman had uncovered. When Damon swore softly, Griff said, "With Lisa Benbow back home there's nothing that can bother me now."

Damon also had more news. He told Griff about Leithbut being found and about the Comanches.

When Griff had washed and shaved and put on a clean shirt, he soberly examined the mail he had thrown on his bunk. There were bills and more bills. But there was one envelope postmarked Austin. It was from Maydelle.

After a stiffly formal opening, she wrote, *The major died Sunday night. He never did stop drinking. Reckon you won't fancy having a woman like me for a partner, but you got no choice. The major left Chainlink to me and you equal. His lawyer in Virginia City wrote that his silver stocks was wiped out. Reckon that helped kill him. I'll be home directly because the money's all gone. Love, Maydelle.*

For a long moment he stared out the window where men were riding in, swinging down from tired horses. Other men were riding out. There was dust and the clatter made by loose horses in the corral, and the ring of iron on iron down at the blacksmith shop. Life went on.

But Major Clay was dead. He tried to feel sad. But how could you weep for a man who had deliberately thrown his life away? Yet he had liked the major. And God knew the major had given him this big chance in life.

A sharp warning surged through him and he reread the part of the letter that told of the major's silver holdings being wiped out. That meant there was no money with which to pay the men, no money for bills. Some cattle would have to be sold off.

He heard the pound of his heart. He was half owner of Chainlink, if Maydelle could be believed. And why not? He looked at the letter. *I'll be home directly*—Home. That meant she intended to live here at Chainlink?

Folding the letter, he jammed it into his pocket. He decided to say nothing to Damon about the major's passing until he had time to think things out. There was no telling how the men might react to this somber news. They might quit if Griff couldn't pay up their back salaries. He knew riders might grumble a little but would hold onto their jobs when working for an irresponsible man like the major. As long as they felt that one day in the near future he would benevolently agree to pay them up.

On the way to Del Carmen the full realization that Milo Clay was gone hit him. In a way he blamed himself. Maybe if he hadn't suggested the major take Maydelle and go away he'd have become interested in Chainlink, and found a substitute in hard work for his drinking. And then again maybe not.

Well, one thing for sure, Griff thought. The major had had a few extra years that would have been denied him if at the close of the war Lieutenant Griffith Jordan had not ridden through his own ranks, the flat of a saber driving a rifle squad out of position, and saved his life.

Dismounting in front of the Benbow house at the east end of town, he went through the gate in the picket fence and climbed the porch steps. His sorrow at the major's passing was dimmed somewhat as he thought of seeing Lisa once again.

The front door opened suddenly. Clyde Benbow, wearing a sweat-stained shirt, lines of pressure on his face, said, "What do you want here, Jordan?"

Griff fought down an urge to turn his back on Benbow. "Lisa came out to Chainlink. I was gone. She left word that she was coming back here."

Some of the venom dropped from Benbow's

voice as he said, "Lisa isn't here. She hasn't come home."

Griff tried to deny the cold edge of fear that rimmed his heart. "Maybe she's visiting friends."

"Her horse is gone. Lisa wouldn't ride to visit friends in town. She'd walk. She likes to walk."

"My God," Griff said, "you don't think the Comanches—"

Benbow's mouth went hard. "What made you say Comanches?"

"Leithbut and the Oakum boys. I understand their bodies were found. Scalped."

"That's right." Benbow looked over his shoulder into the house as if this were very important. Griff Jordan slowly let out his breath and stared hard at Benbow.

When Benbow faced around again, he fairly shouted, "What the hell you looking at me that way for!"

Griff swallowed the suspicion that had darkened his eyes. "You sure your sister isn't home?"

Mention of Lisa caused Benbow to lose his belligerence again. He showed a genuine concern for her safety. He said he'd gone next

234

door to ask a neighbor if Lisa had been seen. "I heard Lisa got in this morning," Benbow said. "When she wasn't home when I got here it worried me. The neighbor said she rode out right after she got in town. She hasn't come back."

Griff turned to go down the porch steps and Benbow said, "Where you going, Jordan?"

Griff looked back at the taut, worried face. He saw the big gun riding against the hip bone. He thought of his own right arm with the bullet scar that had slowed his fingers.

"I'll go see Sam Enright," Griff said. "We better get a posse in the saddle and go look for her."

Benbow caught him at the bottom step. "Wait—" He licked his lips and there was fear for Lisa's safety and also the look of a desperate man in his eyes. "Jordan, I've got me a godawful feeling where she is."

"Tell me, man!"

"I come to within five miles or so of town with George Wheat today. Lisa could have been riding back from your place about the time George headed back to the river—"

"He wouldn't dare touch her!" Griff said, but

there was an edge of worry in his voice. "Would he?"

"He eats and sleeps and drinks Lisa. I had to run him out once, he got to be such a pest."

"And then you took him back," Griff said quietly. "Because I'd hired him in Tucson. And maybe he had some information to sell you. Such as Leithbut—"

Benbow appeared not to hear. He was heading along the walk. "I'm going after Lisa," he said over his shoulder. "I could use some help. You want to come?"

Griff came to the gate. "You ride ahead of me at all times and I'll come. But remember this, Benbow. If this is a deal like that ambush you had set up in Mexico—"

"I dunno what you mean."

"If you've used your sister to trigger a trap for me, you'll never live."

"There's only one damn thing in the world for me, and that's Lisa!"

"That's what everybody says. And it's the only reason I'm going with you. I want to find her as bad as you do."

They went riding south, their animosity buried in a common cause. Even though he sensed Benbow was desperately concerned for

236

Lisa's safety, Griff never let the man get behind him. He always kept Benbow where he could watch him. After the day when he had lost his gun in the fight with George Wheat, he had vowed to carry a spare. When he no longer carried the shotgun for protection, he had taken to wearing not only his belt gun but a revolver under his shirt. Leaving the front of his shirt unbuttoned, he rode mile after mile, left hand gripping the reins, right touching the butt of the gun. If Benbow noticed this he gave no sign.

As darkness came they watered their horses. Then they pushed on. Griff doubled his vigilance, now that only an early moon could warn him of any overt attempt by Benbow on his life. They were in the Chisos where ridges made irregular patterns against the starry sky.

"What makes you think he'll bring her down here?" Griff asked when they were moving single file through a narrow canyon. They had followed the tracks of two riders heading south, but lost them in the darkness.

"There's a shack south of here where Wheat holes up," Benbow said. "I'm playing a hunch. I hope to God I'm right."

Griff kept the shadowed back in plain view

at all times. When they crested a ridge and the trail dropped sharply, and Benbow was momentarily out of sight, Griff drew the revolver from under his shirt. He spurred his horse. But Benbow made no attempt at treachery.

Benbow suddenly drew rein and Griff's horse had to swerve aside to keep from piling into the other mount. Benbow held up his right hand in a signal for silence. And then Griff saw it. A cherry bloom of campfire glow a quarter of a mile ahead.

"George didn't make it to the shack," Benbow said.

"Might be them. Might be a cow camp."

As they watched, something moved and a huge shadow was thrown against a cliff wall. "George Wheat," Benbow said through his teeth.

"Any man is big when he throws a shadow."

"We'll split up," Benbow said tensely. "You come in from the east. I'll go straight ahead. I'll whistle and that'll be the signal to cut down on Wheat."

"Providing it is him," Griff said. "But you're wrong on two counts, Benbow."

"Yeah?" Benbow's voice was taut with suspicion.

"First, we're not splitting up. I don't intend to let you out of my sight."

Benbow swore. His horse stomped and shook its head and bit chains rattled softly in the darkness.

"And we're not cutting down on George Wheat," Griff said grimly. "I want him alive. If he's hurt Lisa I'll heel-drag him clear to Chihuahua City."

"Suit yourself," Benbow said gruffly, and they swung down. They left their horses and their spurs. Gripping rifles, they made ready to move up on the camp.

"You first," Griff said, when Benbow stood aside.

Benbow moved off through the darkness, skirting mesquites. They gauged the wind so as to come up in such a way the camp horses wouldn't catch their scent.

As they cautiously made their way forward Griff saw that it was indeed George Wheat, sitting cross-legged on the ground. He was turning meat over the coals of a fire. It smelled like rabbit. Lisa was there, too, huddled on the ground. Her hands were free, for she was gesturing angrily at Wheat. But her ankles seemed tied.

They moved slower now, parting twigs, bellying along the ground. Once Wheat's big head jerked up and he stared off into the darkness. Griff had him in his sights. If Wheat heard them there was no telling what he might do. He might even kill Lisa. A man crazy enough to kidnap a woman in this country was capable of almost any act.

Wheat went back to his cooking. The savory odor of roasted meat reached Griff and he was reminded that save for a cold breakfast he'd had no food this day.

They rested in the brush so close they could hear voices. There were three horses staked off beyond the rim of light made by the campfire; Lisa's pinto, a big Morgan and a pack mule.

Lisa said, "George, you're mad to think you can get away with this."

"I been in love with you a long time. Why else you think I'd let your brother whip me bloody with that bent nail in a rope? Why else you think I'd come back like a whipped dog and let him hire me again?"

"Clyde will kill you for this, George. Cut me loose and I'll say nothing about it."

Wheat shook his big head slowly from side to side. He broke off a piece of the meat from the roasting rabbit and passed it to Lisa. She refused to take it. She was fumbling with the ropes knotted about her ankles. But they were evidently tied so tight that she could not loosen them.

Griff moved forward again, cautiously, hardly daring to draw breath.

"If a posse comes," Lisa said, with no apparent fear in her voice, "Enright might not be able to hold them in. They'd hang you."

"I mean you no harm, I told you that already." Wheat was sitting on his heels, and now he moved around so he could see the firelight on her golden head. "I aim to marry you, Lisa."

"I'll never agree to that!"

"I know a place in Mexico. I'll leave you there with a woman I know. Then I'll come back and get my money—"

"What money, George?" When he didn't answer, she said, "Is that what was in those sacks you buried in the canyon?"

"We'll live, Lisa. Live real good. You'll be proud to be my wife."

Griff crept nearer, so intent on watching Lisa that he no longer kept his eye on Benbow. And Benbow was gone, slipping off to the left. Griff could hear the faint sounds made as he crawled. Lisa's pinto caught the scent of man or heard Benbow's movement. It threw up its head.

Wheat went over to where Lisa sat on the ground. Suddenly he caught her under the arms and jerked her erect and stepped behind her, crouching, so that only a wedge of his face washed by firelight, showed above her shoulder. Yes, her ankles were tied. Griff could see that clearly now.

"That you out there, Clyde?" Wheat suddenly cried.

"Yes, damn you, it's Clyde!" Benbow was on his feet, aiming a rifle and Griff screamed, "No, you fool, you might hit Lisa!"

Wheat yelled, "I'll tell everything, Clyde! Remember the letter—"

A crashing rifle broke off Wheat's frantic utterance. He fell and so did Lisa. For a cold moment Griff thought Benbow's bullet had gone through the girl and entered Wheat's body. The horses were jumping at their stake ropes. Firelight made crazy patterns against the cliff wall.

Griff sprang forward and pulled Lisa clear of the big man thrashing on the ground. And as

242

he did so there was a second shot and Wheat lay still.

Lisa was huddled on the ground, sobbing with relief and fear and shock.

While Benbow, rifle in hand, stood staring down at the dead George Wheat, Griff freed Lisa's ankles. He heard Benbow mutter, "He doesn't have a Mex gal. I'll bet anything he doesn't."

Griff got up, making no sense out of Benbow's words. "You risked Lisa's life!" he accused. "Or did you know you had to shut Wheat up? Before he said what he was trying to say!"

Benbow turned slowly and lifted the rifle, the barrel slightly above and to the left of Lisa's head. He centered the weapon on Griff's chest. "You been the thorn in my blanket too long, Jordan—"

Lisa, sitting on the ground, reached up and grabbed the barrel of the rifle and the bullet instead of crashing into Griff Jordan, went whistling off into the mesquites. With his stiffened fingers Griff drew his revolver.

But Lisa was up, weeping. "Clyde, don't let your temper run away with you. Please." Then, turning, she ran into Griff's arms. "I'm so glad you came. I prayed you would, Griff. I rode out to see you this morning—"

"I know, I know." With his free hand he patted her sleek head, staring over her shoulder at Clyde Benbow. In Griff's right hand was a cocked revolver. Benbow was rigid, the rifle still in his hands, glaring at them.

Lisa rattled on, "Then when I left Chainlink I ran into George Wheat. He said Clyde had been hurt and he was taking him some supplies on the pack mule. I rode with him, and then I felt of the canvas bags and I suspected they were coins—He got worried then and buried them. And when I tried to get away he tied me up and—Oh, Griff, you're the most wonderful sight I ever beheld in my life."

"What about the man in Austin? You were going to marry him."

"There was no man," she said, drawing back and looking at him. Then she turned. "Clyde, did you spread a story like that?"

Benbow said coldly, "Come on, Lisa. I'm taking you home."

"We'll all ride together. We'll all be friends now." Lisa gave Benbow an anxious glance. "The three of us—"

"I don't want him for a friend. I don't want the major for a friend."

"You won't have him for a friend, even if you wanted it," Griff said. He told them of the letter from Maydelle saying Major Milo Clay died in Austin.

"I'm so sorry," Lisa said. "I know he was quite ill the last time I saw him."

Benbow stepped forward. "You coming with me, Lisa?"

"Don't go with him," Griff said.

Lisa made her choice. "I'll ride with him, Griff. But come and see me. Soon." She came close and whispered, "Please understand. I know how Clyde is when he gets this way. I don't want trouble between you. I couldn't stand that. There's already been enough."

Griff was about to tell her that Clyde Benbow was not her brother, that he was no kin at all. But she had turned and in a moment was riding out with Benbow, leading the pack mule, and Wheat's horse.

As the sounds of their passing faded Griff stared down at Wheat's body. A poor stupid fool in love with a woman who was a million miles out of his reach.

He had no stomach to bury the body. He'd

tell Sam Enright about it. If the sheriff wanted to come this far south he could bring Wheat to town. It was up to him.

Relieved that Lisa was no longer threatened by Wheat, but hurt that she had decided to ride with Benbow, he turned his horse for Chainlink.

He tried to understand her actions. He guessed she still believed Clyde Benbow could be handled. She didn't realize that he was like an outlaw horse that was a killer and no good on earth.

With the mountain breeze strong against his face, he knew it could only end one way. With Clyde Benbow dead by violence. *Maybe I'm not the one to do it,* Griff thought. *Maybe he'll down me like he did Wheat tonight. But somebody will do it.*

As he came out of the mountains at last he thought of the irony of the major deeding a full share of Chainlink to Griff Jordan, the man who had saved his life. And an equal share to a niece, Maydelle Ashley. And Maydelle did not speak of Clay as her uncle. Only as the major.

With her living at Chainlink, what could he look forward to? He had what he'd always wanted, a solid chunk of a good ranch. Not a quarter interest the major had given him when they started this venture in Virginia City. But a full half interest.

He knew one thing. Maydelle would be a tough partner. She would never let him forget that she had left her bedroom door open. And he hadn't accepted the offer.

She must thoroughly hate him.

19

OCCASIONALLY Benbow and Lisa rested their horses, but that was the only time they stopped. They rode all night and into the next day. It was noon when they arrived at the house in town.

Only when they were in the house together did Lisa break the silence she had maintained all during the ride. She told Benbow how she had seen the major and Maydelle in San Antone. "The major told me why Griff Jordan fought for the North." She went into some detail explaining what the major had told her. Benbow sat on the edge of a table swinging a dusty boot. "You've got to admire a man like that, Clyde," Lisa said. "And I do admire him. I love him."

"He's a turncoat," Benbow said, a sickness in his voice. "You'll never be happy with him." He took a step toward her, his face ugly. "I thought it was always going to be you and me together—"

There was a step on the porch and Benbow

turned and saw Jim Penwade just coming to the door. "Clyde, I just seen you ride in," the owner of the Del Carmen Bar said. "There's a meetin' at my place now. Oh, hello, Miss Lisa. You'll brighten this town a bit now that you're back. Lord knows it's been pretty black these last days."

Lisa came to the door. "What's been the trouble?"

Benbow said, "Nothing," and tried to change the subject. But Lisa was persistent.

Penwade gave a worried shake of his head. "Some things has happened awful fast, Clyde. The sheriff is missin'. And we're worried about Comanches. Maybe Sam run into some of 'em."

"There's been Indian trouble again?" Lisa shared Penwade's worry.

"Well, they was all right a spell back. Then they found Leithbut and the Oakum brothers scalped." While Penwade recited some of the other grim details, Lisa turned slowly and faced her brother. They stood frozen, eyes locked on the other's face. Slowly Lisa went pale. Penwade, not wishing to intrude in what appeared to be shaping up as a bad scene between Clyde and his sister, said, "The meeting, Clyde. I'll tell the boys to hold off till you get there."

He went down the steps and along the walk and through the gate. He looked back once, shaking his head.

Lisa was hunched over as if in pain. She put her two hands palms down on a cherrywood table. She closed her eyes. "Leithbut," she whispered hoarsely. "The money, Clyde. Not a Chicago packing house. Leithbut."

Benbow came to her swiftly and put his hands on her arms and swung her around. "It's Jordan. I didn't want to tell you, but Sam Enright came by here the other day. He said he found a witness who saw Jordan and that one-eyed segundo of his trailing Leithbut and the Oakum boys—"

"What witness?" she demanded coldly.

"Enright never told me. He said he was going to look at a certain shack down by the river. He said if he wasn't back in two days to go looking for him."

"I don't believe you."

She struggled and tried to get away, but his hands were strong and under his fingers her shirt parted. Her face flamed and she said, desperately, "Clyde, let me go!"

250

His face changed. Suddenly he swung her off her feet and into his arms and carried her up the stairs. She hung limp, stunned, unable to comprehend. He carried her into the bedroom and put her down on the bed and held her there. Then she saw in his eyes what he intended to do.

She lay still under the iron bar of his arm. "It's funny, Clyde, but Mr. Goodrich wrote me in Austin. He told me how Poppa found you. But I didn't believe him. I knew he hated you because of Maydelle. And I thought he was trying to get back at you by hurting me."

"Lisa, we'll have everything. Like it was in Poppa's time—"

". . . I didn't believe Goodrich. But now I know."

Suddenly she bit his wrist and as the blood flowed down on the coverlet she sprang aside. But he made a wild grab and caught her.

"You'll hate yourself, Clyde. Every day you live you'll hate yourself."

"We're going to be married."

"You and George Wheat," she said, her lips curling. "Only George said he wouldn't touch me until I agreed to marry him."

"Listen to me. I've loved you ever since the day you took your first step."

"You've never loved anything in your life but Chainlink."

"Lisa—" He crushed her beneath him and as she looked into his eyes she said, "Don't do it, Clyde. If you do I'll go out into the street. I'll tell them what you did to me. I'll tell it, Clyde. So help me God I'll tell it. And they'll hang you for it. You know it just as sure as you're alive this minute."

Slowly his face altered and the hunger in his eyes turned into something else. "I didn't plan it this way, Lisa. I wanted to wait till I had Chainlink back. To tell you that I got it back for you. I thought you'd remember our years together. That you'd love me."

"I loved a brother, Clyde. But that man is dead. Just as sure as you'll be dead in fact, not in memory, if you don't let me up."

"Damn you!" he cried, and his hands pinned her down.

"I'll scream," she threatened.

"I could spoil it for Jordan. That much I can do."

His hand was over her mouth and she tried to use her teeth, but the hand was smothering, pinching in her nostrils. Her body heaved and still the one arm was across her, pinning her.

But in a moment he got up, his face dead white. "You'll come to me. After everything else is over, you'll come to me. Because you have nothing else."

He stormed out of the room. For a long time she sat still in the center of the bed.

Benbow went along the street, intending to get good and drunk at the Del Carmen House. Then he remembered the meeting Penwade had asked him to attend. Could he trust Lisa now? Probably not. She might keep her mouth shut if he didn't move against Jordan. But if he sent a posse down to the river, telling them Enright had said if he didn't return in two days to come and look for him—and if they found his body, and went for Jordan with a rope—Lisa might voice her suspicions of the Leithbut business. And others might believe her. Others might be believing it anyway.

But she might remain silent in order to avoid disgrace. But if he pressed Jordan now—Well, that could come later.

A rider came slowly from the far side of the

stable and reined in. Because the sun was in his eyes Benbow didn't recognize Lawler at first.

Then, when he saw the scarred mouth smiling he felt a premonition of disaster. Lawler swung down and leisurely tied his horse. He came over at a jaunty walk, hat on the back of his head.

"You sorta peeled the skin off me and Macready where it's real tender," Lawler said bluntly, but still smiling.

"Just what's that supposed to mean?" Benbow put a hand on his gun. His nerves had been pressured too much over the past hours to stand much more.

"Don't pull that gun," Lawler advised, "until I have my say."

"Then get at it."

They stood by the stable wall. The sun was warm on Benbow's face, on Lawler's back. "I been months down along the river, Clyde. I ain't had much fun. Now and then George Wheat comes down and says you want us to run off more Chainlink beef. I'm just like a trained horse. I'm gettin' tired of it."

Benbow considered the basis for this open threat and could find none. Lawler was a good hand and usually could be trusted to do any number of dirty jobs. He usually had his hat in his hand when he talked to the Benbows. This was the first time he had ever shown his horns. Something must have given him a lot of confidence all of a sudden.

"Go on, Art," Benbow said, forcing a smile. "I know it's been tough on you boys, but we'll all live good when I get Chainlink back."

"I'm damn disappointed in you, Clyde." Lawler spat insolently, nearly hitting the toe of Benbow's boot. Benbow was within a breath of smashing him in the face.

"When any two-bit stuff come along, you had me and Macready do it. But when you get a chance at some real gold, by damn you don't tell us nothing. Of course Macready's dead now. But I'm still feelin' spring in my knees. I'd like to go to Chihuahua and get a rancho and live fine, Clyde. Real fine."

"That takes money."

"Glad you mentioned that." Lawler's eyes were bright. "Seein' as how I done your back-shootin' for you I figure I oughta be paid real good. I want a slice of that eighty-thousand dollar pie you an' George Wheat got from Leithbut."

Benbow forced himself to say, "Where'd you ever hear a wild story like that?"

"Big stupid George got himself a Mex gal down on the river. But George don't know how to write so he gets this gal to write a letter for him. And if anything happens to George she's supposed to give it to some folks George knows here."

Benbow felt a prickle of ice along the back of his neck. "This don't figure," Benbow said, really at a loss now. "How'd you know George is dead?"

"I didn't. Don't make no mind. I like George better dead." Lawler got confidential. "This Mex gal of George's, she likes me. She can't stand this big horse George so she shows me this letter. I come up from the border real fast, Clyde, to talk to you about it."

The evening stage came hammering up from the west at that moment, wheels and hoofs whipping dust, small boys shouting alongside, the driver yelling more than necessary, making a show out of the arrival.

Making a wheel-locked stop, the stage skidded to a halt in front of the Del Carmen House. Hardly had the dust settled than from the coach stepped a woman, wearing a tall hat

256

with a feather in it. Clyde Benbow remembered something Griff Jordan had said in the Chisos: "*The major is dead.*"

He saw Maydelle go into the hotel, saw people turn and stare at her.

Benbow said, "Art, let's you and me go and have ourselves a drink. This ought to be right interesting. Seeing the town's madam in the Del Carmen House."

"What about that money, Clyde?"

"I was figuring to deal you in all the time. When it happened I couldn't trust Macready. Otherwise I'd have taken you with George when we—" There was no sense in going into details even with Lawler.

Scowling, Lawler hesitated a moment, then trailed along. From the hotel came Maydelle's shrill voice: "If you don't give me a room you'll be sorry. I'll buy this hotel! I'll buy this town! Me and Griff Jordan own Chainlink! You remember that—"

Benbow, coming lightly up the porch steps, removed his hat and forced his best smile. "Maydelle, it's so good to see you back home again."

Maydelle, as well as the crowd on the porch, looked at him as if he had lost his senses.

"Are you trying to say that your uncle is dead?" Benbow sounded genuinely surprised.

"You didn't know, Clyde?" Maydelle said, a momentary softening touching her eyes.

He reached for her arm and led her down the steps and said, "Tell me about it. The major and I had our differences, but I liked him."

"It was whisky killed him." Maydelle walked stiffly at his side, past the groups of staring onlookers.

"I don't blame him for drinking," Benbow said. "Being partner to a turncoat is enough to drive any man to a drunkard's grave."

Maydelle glanced up at him. "You mean that's why he drank? On account of Griff Jordan? I—I always thought he drank on account of me."

"I don't envy you being a partner to Griff Jordan," Benbow said seriously. "A man who'd go to war against his own brother." He lifted his hands, let them fall. "No telling what he might do."

Maydelle said nothing. They kept walking, passing shops where people stared curiously from windows, some of them indignant.

"You shouldn't have tried to shame me by all the things you did," Benbow said. "I wanted to marry you. After Tom was killed I was my own man."

"Tom kept you and me from marrying?" she asked.

He nodded, putting bitterness in his eyes. "Then after Tom died, you acted—Well, a man doesn't like to think that a woman he was in love with did all the things you did."

Her lower lip trembled. "Oh, Clyde, I'm so ashamed. When I saw Lisa in San Antone she was so nice to me and I—The major died the day she left. I—I just couldn't stand it there. I had to come home."

"Sure you did," Benbow said. "You're home now."

They had reached the west end of town where the walk ended in brush. Maydelle faced him, the hurt gone from her eyes now. "You're no good, Clyde," she said softly. "You fooled me for a bit because you said the things I wanted to hear. But I hate Griff Jordan almost as much as you do."

He saw the boldness back in her eye and he had the uncomfortable feeling that the front door of a parlor house had just closed against his back.

Later, when he got back to the house, he

found a note from Lisa saying she had moved to the hotel. She didn't want to see him at all.

Benbow clenched a fist. "No matter what I've got to do," he said to the empty house, "I'll have her. In the long run I'll have her."

After a hectic day and a long talk with Lawler, Benbow got the word he wanted. Lawler returned from a scouting expedition. "Chainlink crew is at roundup camp. Nobody at headquarters but Jordan and that one-eyed segundo of his."

"This time has got to be it," Benbow said. "No mistakes this time."

"I don't like havin' a woman along," Lawler said, when Benbow explained his plan.

"She's got every right to be there, Art. Every right."

20

THE next morning Griff and Ed Damon were getting ready to ride out to the roundup camp that had been established when Lisa Benbow, dressed in a riding skirt came across the clearing. She dismounted and stood by her horse, looking so whipped that Griff thought at first she might be ill.

Leaving Damon by the bunkhouse, Griff hurried toward her. "Lisa, what's the matter?"

She put a forearm across her eyes. "Clyde and Maydelle were married this morning."

"Oh, God no!"

"I thought you should know, Griff."

He clenched his hands. "After what he did to her. How could she—"

"The main thing is that Clyde has what he's sworn to get. Chainlink."

"He hasn't got it yet," Griff said in a terrible voice.

"He has his foot in the door. As Maydelle's husband—" Then she told him that Clyde

261

Benbow wasn't her brother. But she didn't tell him what Clyde had tried to do.

"For a long time I've sensed something odd about him," Lisa went on. "But I pretended it didn't exist. That this feeling he showed for me was—well, brother and sister."

"Lisa, I—"

"Hear me out, Griff. I want you to know I care nothing for him. He—he killed whatever respect I ever had for him. He's going to die, Griff. But I don't want to be here to see it. Please, not that."

"He was born to die violently."

"If you shot him—Well, if he died with your bullet in him I'd stay with you. If you want me."

"Want you? Of course I want you—" His hands reached for her, but she backed away.

"Clyde is going to be hanged. I don't want to be in Texas when it happens."

"Hanged for what?" he asked, but he knew.

"Leithbut. I'm going to tell Sam Enright. And I suppose I'll have to testify. After the verdict is brought in, I want you to take me away. Before—it happens."

"You still have some feeling for him."

She shook her head. "I'm thinking of Poppa.

He was a strange man, cruel in a lot of ways. He loved Clyde more than any of us. But there was a gentle side to Poppa that no one ever knew but me. And he realized too late what Clyde was. Poppa was sick and he gambled a lot. And when he lost—Well, he took his own life. But I can see now it was really Clyde that killed him. Clyde stole from Poppa. And that broke Poppa's heart. I—I stayed awake last night, thinking. A lot of things have become clear."

"Did Clyde hurt you?" he asked suddenly. "Physically, I mean?"

"No." She avoided looking at him. "Chain-link has brought happiness to no one," she said.

"It can bring happiness to us."

"Why here in Texas? Why not someplace else?"

"I love Texas."

"And yet you didn't fight for it—" Her mouth trembled, and she said quickly, "Oh, Griff, I'm sorry."

He felt old and empty. "It would be between us for the rest of our lives, Lisa. Turncoat."

"I didn't mean it that way, Griff." She put a hand to her face. "I want you—I want us to get out of Texas! Sell your half of Chainlink. There'll be somebody to buy it."

"But I've gambled everything to come back to Texas."

"How will it be for our children, Griff? That's the important part."

He felt a rush of warmth through his whole being.

"Maybe you're right." He looked around the yard at the buildings of Chainlink headquarters. "Maybe a man's last chance isn't so important. Maybe there's always another chance, a better one if a man will only seek it out."

"Oh, Griff, you will leave here?"

"I thought maybe after a few years people would forget the war. But instead of dying it grows. Maybe someday there'll be no bitterness. But now—" He gave her a wan smile. "But I had to try it. And in trying it I found you."

She was in his arms then. He was dimly aware of the clatter of wagon wheels, of an approaching team's muffled steps in dust. But he had no thoughts for anything but this girl. She found his mouth and after a moment she drew back.

"I didn't bite you this time, Griff."

"Why the other time?"

"Because I wanted you and I was scared. I thought I had to fight back—"

From over by the bunkhouse Ed Damon cried, "Company comin', Griff!"

Griff turned, seeing a buggy pulled up across the yard. Maydelle sat on the seat, holding her plumed hat with one hand. Clyde Benbow, dressed in a black suit, stepped down. He removed his coat and laid it across the seat, for the day was warm. His shirt was startlingly white. Around his waist was cinched a holstered revolver. The brim of his black hat was pulled low.

He came slowly across the yard and halted a few feet away.

Lisa clung to Griff's arm. "It's all over, Clyde. Don't try anything now. Nothing you can say or do will part us."

"Lisa, get away from him," Benbow said.

"No."

"Art," Benbow called. "When I give the word, drop him!"

With a scream of rage Lisa lunged at Benbow. He caught her by the wrists and flung her roughly aside so that she rolled over and over across the rocky ground, her skirts flying. Spooked by this apparition, the buggy team lunged into harness with such suddenness that Maydelle, half-standing in rigid fear at what might happen before her eyes, was tumbled out of the seat. The team turned sharply and skidded the buggy into the corral fence, shattering one wheel and the tongue, so that the team pulled free and went racing out onto the flats beyond the house.

Art Lawler had suddenly appeared at the far side of the barn, the horse he had ridden up drifting away. Ed Damon, who had let Lawler ride up on his blind side, now whirled, his single eye glittering.

"Clear out!" he ordered Lawler.

Maydelle, sitting up on the ground, cried, "Clyde, you promised there'd be no shootin'!"

When Lawler didn't move, Damon whirled and snatched up a rifle that was leaning against the bunkhouse wall.

Lawler took his time, aiming his revolver. He shot Damon in the chest, and as the man lurched, shot him again.

Lisa lay where she had fallen and a fear for her safety lurched through Griff. She had been flung so hard to the ground by Benbow that she seemed unconscious. She lay on her stomach, her head turned sideways. But the side of her face Griff might have seen was covered by her wild pale hair.

He saw Benbow at a crouch now, feet solidly planted. Hand moving toward the belt, snapping up. And Griff stood as if frozen. Where was the magic, the instinct that had saved him that day with Keller? Gone. Gone forever in the torn ligaments of a shattered arm. And the man who had ruined the arm now at his back. Lawler with the scarred mouth. He could hear Lawler angling in.

"George Wheat tried to kill you the day he saw you put your hands on Lisa!" Benbow was shouting. "I'll make sure of the job."

Griff moved desperately, falling away. Hearing the hammer of the slug as it drove solidly into the mud wall at his back. He saw the trail of muzzle smoke as Benbow shifted the weapon to trail his moving target.

"Art, get him!" Benbow yelled.

Art Lawler came in close, grinning, wanting to see it done close up. Wanting to see the knowledge of death in the eyes of the man he wanted to kill. Wanting to read it up close. Griff pivoted and his two hands caught Lawler's gun wrist and he dragged Lawler to the ground with him. Lawler fired into the Texas hard pan, angered, a little scared.

Benbow was holding his fire because Lawler was right in line. Then he evidently decided to shoot anyway. Streak of red flame, jarring smash of lead into Lawler's body. And Lawler dying with the scream of double-cross on his lips.

Griff, having felt the slam of the bullet into Lawler, turned loose of the man. He rolled, rolled, and came up with dust in his eyes and the scream of bullets in his ears. And saw Benbow, feet widespread, hat gone, eyes wide. Firing. Erratic firing. A nervous man shooting. Trying to end something. His nerves gone, wanting only to kill finally and completely. Jerking his gun when it should be steady.

And Griff, drawing his gun. Stiffened fingers around the cool walnut grips. A thumb clumsily drawing back the hammer. Letting it fall.

Because Griff was on his knees, trying to gain his feet as he fired, the shot went wild. As wild and erratic as Benbow's firing. Then Benbow, going white, looking at the gun in his hand, then flinging it. Griff ducking as the empty gun clubbed his hat from his head and went skating across the yard.

Benbow sprinted to the fallen one-eyed Ed Damon. He grabbed Damon's rifle and swung around, as Griff staggered to his feet. Griff knew then that he had been hit. By that first bullet Benbow had fired. Yes, that was it. Not stiffened fingers alone that did not respond. Not that alone. No, the front of his shirt was wet and he felt the delayed shock of a bullet. He was falling. If only he had three more hands. Three more hands to steady the right hand holding the gun. The gun that weighed more than a full grown cow.

And Benbow, sensing that he had his man at last. Taking his time now. Sighting his rifle. And Griff thumbing desperately. Feeling the gun jump in his hand. Seeing the surprise on Benbow's face. Seeing the pattern of dust move up Benbow's body from the belt line. Small puffs of dust and when the dust instantly blew away, seeing the holes A crazy zig zag pattern up Benbow's front, from the silver buckle to his chin. And then the chin was gone.

Griff lay flat in the dust. He could move only his head. He looked. Benbow lay on an elbow, staring at the pattern made by his own blood in the dust. And then with a sigh he fell across it and was still.

Griff floundered over on his back like a hooked fish. "Lisa!" His voice was far away. So far away.

And Lisa crawling to him across the ground. Dazed. Her hair loose about her face. A smudge of dust on one cheek. A cut on her right temple where her head had struck a stone.

The two women got him into the house and Maydelle rode a saddler, her skirts flying, all the way to Del Carmen to fetch Doc Purcell.

Later, Doc, his bald head gleaming in lamp-light said, "You just can't kill a man like Griff Jordan."

A week later some men from town rode by to say that they had found Enright's body. After rounding up some suspected rustlers along the river, they put two and two together. Enright's body had been found near a shack where George Wheat had holed up for several months. Either Wheat or Benbow had likely shot Enright.

Griff was sitting on the porch, wrapped in a blanket, his chest still heavily bandaged. He looked pale and drawn.

The men from town were polite to Lisa, cool to Griff. When they had given their infor-mation, they rode out.

Griff caught Lisa's hand. "Where do you want to go?"

"Go?"

"You said you wanted to leave Texas."

"The leaving will be done by Maydelle. She's gone. A respectable widow woman now. I hope she finds some happiness. I told her we'd have to haul in a mighty short rope, as Poppa used to say, until we get things on a paying basis. But I said to let us know where she was and that she would always have her share of the profits. I told her that in a year or two maybe we could buy her out."

"But you said you didn't want to stay here."

She put her arm across his shoulders and sat on the arm of the chair. "I had a long talk with Doc Purcell. He said you tried to run once. And you weren't happy."

"You said the children would suffer."

"Where in this world can you find a place where there is no suffering? There's no paradise. You did what you thought was right in the war. What else can a man do? Except do what he thinks is right."

"That sounds like Doc again."

"I was born in this house, Griff. I want my children to be born here."

271

"But you said the place had given no one happiness."

She did not answer. "I sent word with Doc to tell some of the men in town where George Wheat buried his share of the Leithbut money. I don't suppose we'll ever find Clyde's share."

"Chainlink whipped Clyde and it helped whip the major," Griff said, feeling a return of confidence he had not experienced since that bullet had shattered his breastbone. "It won't whip us."

"Speaking of children, as we were a moment ago," Lisa said with a sly smile, "if you don't marry me people will begin to talk."

"We could ride to town today."

"You're not well enough. Besides, Doc said there was a traveling sky pilot in Del Carmen. He's coming out here this afternoon."

"Another ambush," Griff said. "And I walked right into it."

Other titles in the
Linford Western Library:

SUNDANCE: SILENT ENEMY
by John Benteen

Both the Indians and the U.S. Cavalry were being victimized. A lone crazed Cheyenne was on a personal war path against both sides. They needed to pit one man against one crazed Indian. That man was Sundance.

LASSITER
by Jack Slade

Lassiter wasn't the kind of man to listen to reason. Cross him once and he'd hold a grudge for years to come—if he let you live that long. But he was no crueler than the men he had killed, and he had never killed a man who didn't need killing.

LAST STAGE TO GOMORRAH
by Barry Cord

Jeff Carter, tough ex-riverboat gambler, now had himself a horse ranch that kept him free from gunfights and card games. Until Sturvesant of Wells Fargo showed up. Jeff owed him a favour and Sturvesant wanted it paid up. All he had to do was to go to Gomorrah and recover a quarter of a million dollars stolen from a stagecoach!

McALLISTER ON THE COMANCHE CROSSING
by Matt Chisholm

The Comanche, deadly warriors and the finest horsemen in the world, reckon McAllister owes them a life—and the trail is soaked with the blood of the men who had tried to outrun them before.

QUICK-TRIGGER COUNTRY
by Clem Colt

Turkey Red hooked up with Curly Bill Graham's outlaw crew and soon made a name for himself. But wholesale murder was out of Turk's line, so when range war flared he bucked the whole border gang alone . . .

PISTOL LAW
by Paul Evan Lehman

Lance Jones came back to Mustang for just one thing—Revenge! Revenge on the people who had him thrown in jail; on the crooked marshal; on the human vulture who had already taken over the town. Now it was Lance's turn . . .

GUNSLINGER'S RANGE
by Jackson Cole

Three escaped convicts are out for revenge. They won't rest until they put a bullet through the head of the dirty snake who locked them behind bars.

RUSTLER'S TRAIL
by Lee Floren

Jim Carlin knew he would have to stand up and fight because he had staked his claim right in the middle of Big Ike Outland's best grass. Jim also had a score to settle with his renegade brother.

Larry and Stretch:
THE TRUTH ABOUT SNAKE RIDGE
by Marshall Grover

The troubleshooters came to San Cristobal to help the needy. For Larry and Stretch the turmoil began with a brawl, then an ambush, and then another attempt on their lives—all in one day.

CAMPAIGNING
by Jim Miller

Ambushed on the Santa Fe trail, Sean Callahan is saved from dying by two Indian strangers. Then the trio is joined by a former slave called Hannibal. But there'll be more lead and arrows flying before the band join the legendary Kit Carson in his campaign against the Comanches.

WOLF DOG RANGE
by Lee Floren

Montana was big country, but not big enough for a ruthless land-grabber like Will Ardery. He would stop at nothing, unless something stopped him first—like a bullet from Pete Manly's gun.

Larry and Stretch: DEVIL'S DINERO
by Marshall Grover

Plagued by remorse, a rich old reprobate hired the Texas Troubleshooters to deliver a fortune in greenbacks to each of his victims. Even before Larry and Stretch rode out of Cheyenne, a traitor was selling the secret and the hunt was on.

DONOVAN
by Elmer Kelton

Donovan was supposed to be dead. The town had buried him years before when Uncle Joe Vickers had fired off both barrels of a shotgun into the vicious outlaw's face as he was escaping from jail. Now Uncle Joe had been shot—in just the same way.

CODE OF THE GUN
by Gordon D. Shirreffs

MacLean came riding home with saddle-tramp written all over him, but sewn in his shirt-lining was an Arizona Ranger's star. MacLean had his own personal score to settle—in blood and violence!

LUCK

n

nd quick wi

their names a

ng. Parker wa

was his life—or hi

death . . .

ORPHAN'S PREFERRED
by Jim Miller

A boy in a hurry to be a man, Sean Callahan
answers the call of the Pony Express. With
a little help from his Uncle Jim and the Navy
Colt .36, Sean fights Indians and outlaws to
get the mail through.